Prey of Desire

JC Gatlin

PREY OF DESIRE
Copyright © November 2013 by JC Gatlin

ISBN-10: 0615961053
ISBN-13: 978-0615961057
Cover images from Canstock Photography, image # csp9716326 and csp1339663

For Lisa Millard

Prologue

Friday, May 24, 1974
11:32 PM

    Beneath a brilliant swirl of stars, the Black
Moon Forest stood like an impenetrable wall of
twisted pines, cypress trees and thatch, and from
deep within its bowels came an eighteen year old
man, running bloody and scared.

    Brian Williams, the popular senior on the varsity
wrestling team and son of the wealthy state governor,
was neither aware nor cared that he was covered
only by his underwear, still wet and torn from a frantic
rage through the hushed swamp. His vulnerable feet
were bleeding and left a splattering red trail behind
him. And, in his bare arms, he held the lifeless,

naked body of his girlfriend.

He ran faster out of the thorny brush, holding her tightly to him, struggling to warm her skin.

Directly ahead, outlined in the night, Brian could make out a farmhouse. Its black windows reflected moonlight like a warning beacon. As he approached, he fell to his knees and screamed for help. He nearly dropped the naked girl, but tightened his grip then screamed again, a wail more agonizing than before.

Lights flipped on inside and, from the deep shadows of the porch, the screen door opened. Someone approached. Clothed in a blue robe and night slippers, a man stepped to the edge. He paused there with an expression of surprise on his face. It turned to shock, then to unimaginable horror.

Brian's eyes met the young father's as he struggled to hold Bonnie upright. Her skin was now pale and bloated, her long black hair matted and stuck to her head. She wasn't breathing, and it was his fault. He tightened his grip on her body and trembled, sobbing uncontrollably.

"Help her," Brian cried. "Please."

Her father leapt from the porch edge and raced toward them. Brian watched him approach.

"W-we were at the lake when something happened." The boy could barely speak. "She just disappeared under the water and I - I - I didn't know what to do..." He coughed, expelling water from his own strained lungs.

The father knelt in front of them. He reached out and touched his daughter's arm, then her face.

He immediately removed his robe and placed it over Bonnie's bare shoulders, covering her breasts.

He didn't ask what happened, or how, or why. A dead stillness had overcome him, and he said simply, quietly, "We need to get her inside."

Brian shook his head, looking at his girlfriend's body, then at the stoic father, then back at the body. "S-Shouldn't we get her to the hospital? Don't we need to do something? Call someb..."

"We need to get her inside," he said again.

Brian didn't know what to do. Everything around him seemed to be moving in slow motion. The ground was spinning; stars above him blinked out of existence. There were crickets chirping and then silence, then chirping.

"Young man," the father said again for a third time. "We need to get her inside."

Cringing, Brian shifted and grabbed hold of her legs. The father slipped his arms around her torso, lifting her up. Together, they carried her through the dark as her arms dragged across the damp grass. The robe fell away. They trampled it as they brought her to the porch, stepped up and opened the screen door. They carried her inside.

Laying her on the kitchen table, the father covered her bare body with the table cloth. Her eyes rolled open and, with every move, water trickled from her mouth and nose.

Brian lost control.

"We need to call somebody." He brought his hands up to his temples and turned away. His fingers ran up his forehead and through his wet hair, pulling and tugging at it. He paced around the kitchen. "We got to do something for her. Tell somebody."

Without a word, Bonnie's father walked away. Brian watched him.

"What are you doing?" He stopped pacing. "We can call my Dad. He'll know what to do."

The father returned to the kitchen with his tool box. He set it on the table next to Bonnie. Opening it, he took out a hammer and a tape measure. There were other tools, and he fumbled through them, searching.

"Are you listening to me?" Brian yelled, fighting back tears. "My dad, he knows the best doctors. He can help. We gotta do somethin' for her."

The stoic father paused, turning his head. His eyes pierced the teenage boy with sharp, brutal stabs. He turned back to his task, removing nails and a level. He found a spiked awl.

"What are you doing? This is crazy." Brian stepped closer to Bonnie's corpse; his own wet, near-naked body trembled. He was crying now. Unable to comprehend what was happening, he touched her hand dangling over the table and held it tightly in his own. Her palm felt like clay and her fingers like rubber. He shut her eyes as tears rolled down his cheeks. He looked back at her father.

The man lunged forward and jabbed the spiked awl into Brian's right eye.

It was one, swift motion.

The father stepped back as Brian's body twitched violently, his hands flailing toward the wood handle sticking out of his eye socket and pressing against his nose. A second later, he collapsed to the floor.

The father stood there and watched the teenager die, then turned to his daughter's corpse.

"Oh, Bonnie," he whispered. "If you forget me, there's something I want you to know..."

JC Gatlin

25 years later...

JC Gatlin

1

If You Forget Me...

Friday, December 31, 1999
7:10 PM

He may have been the only person in the entire world alone on this New Year's Eve. He sure felt like it.

Like any average twenty-year-old boy with a broken heart, Ross McGuire stood in the parking lot of the Flying J Truck Stop, twenty miles north of Tampa, Florida, at a pay phone. He didn't want to be alone. He pressed the silver buttons with frantic urgency, but paused before hitting the last digit. *What was he going to say? Would she even accept his call?* It had been three weeks, four days and sixteen hours since he pulled his Camero to the side of the road, let her out and drove off, leaving her sobbing in the rearview mirror.

Three weeks, four days and sixteen hours.

A semi truck pulled into the parking lot, grumbling loudly as it rolled past the frail phone booth. Ross slammed down the receiver. Turning to his blue Camero parked a few feet away, he made the decision: He was leaving. For good. *She* called off the engagement; not him. *She* ended this relationship; not him. It was time to move on.

And it was the perfect time to do so. It was about to become a new year. A new century. Time to start a new chapter of his life.

With keys in hand, he shook his head and looked out at the dark parking lot. The semi pulled around and slowed. Brakes squealed as steam released above the tires. Halting, the large truck blocked his view of the storefront and engulfed him in deep shadows. Almost as if it was cutting him off from the world.

Standing in inky blackness, Ross paused. Or, more accurately, he was stopped by the weight of a small diamond ring in his shirt's breast pocket. He removed it and held it in his hands for several seconds.

Despite the oppressing shadow of the semi, the small Solitaire diamond sparkled, reflecting the swirling starlight above him. He really loved this ring. Its thin band was two-toned, and contained a small, studded diamond indicating elegance and intricacy. To him, this symbol truly represented Kimberly, the love of his life. He picked it out nearly two years ago,

and had saved and scrimped and sacrificed to buy it.
When he finally proposed and slipped the ring on her
finger, her reaction was a resounding, "Yes!"

Barely twenty-four hours later, she gave it back.
In a fit of rage, he'd pulled off the highway and left
her standing at the gravel shoulder. Their relationship
was over.

Or was it? Could he ever really stop? They had
their ups and downs; he knew that. He admitted that
he'd hurt her. And, he really did love her. Squeezing
the ring in his palm, he returned to the phone booth
and dialed her number. All seven digits this time.

The line rang.

He waited.

It rang again. A female voice answered on the
other end.

Before Ross could respond, a hand wrapped
around his throat, cutting off his windpipe. Shocked,
he struggled and flailed his arms. The grip tightened
and a second later he felt a sharp pain in his right
eye. The thin spiked awl penetrated his upper eye
cavity, through the skull and pierced his brain. Ross
slumped forward, dead.

The diamond engagement ring dropped from
his palm and clinked onto the pavement just beyond
the phone booth. The black handset hung wildly
above Ross' body as his girlfriend's voice rippled
through the receiver.

"Hello...?"

A man leaned down and picked up the ring,
then nodded toward the phone booth. Reaching out,
he picked up the swaying handset and listened

to the woman on the other end.

"Hello?" she asked again. *"Is someone there?"*
He hung up the phone.

"Oh, Kimberly," he whispered. "If you forget me,
there's something I want you to know..."

* * * * * * *

"Hello...?" she had asked into the phone in her
living room. "Is someone there?" But there was no
answer. She could hear breathing, then a muffled
uuummppfff. The phone clicked and the line went
dead.

Kimberly Bradford thought little more about it
and hung up the phone.

It was New Year's Eve, the dawn of a new
century, and her first evening out since getting
dumped three weeks, four days and 16 hours ago.
Nothing was going the way she expected. She was
running late for a blind date she'd been reluctant to
accept in the first place. Then the kitchen garbage
disposal exploded and drenched her evening gown
with black muddy grime, making her even later. The
landlord said he'd be right over to fix it, but Kim
couldn't wait. She grabbed the nearest towel and ran
next door with Zeus, her Doberman, to her best
friend's townhome.

Now, an hour later, Kim was borrowing evening
wear from a woman with a fashion sense somewhat
more liberal than her own. To add insult to injury, she
was having a bad hair day.

She walked to the bedroom mirror and turned, carefully studying the low-cut, blood red gown with leopard print breasts. She shook her head, mortified.

"Don't you have something black?" she asked, turning away from the mirror. "How about that dinner jacket you wore last week?"

"You look fine." Her friend's reply was muffled behind the bathroom door, which was slightly ajar with the shower running. Kim shook her head.

"I don't think so. Reds just not my color..."

The bathroom door opened wider and Mallory poked her head out, glancing at Kim. At twenty-two, Kim was a college student at Stillwater University and, as Mallory liked to describe her, a "book worm." Kim had only one boyfriend her entire life - an aimless but incredibly good looking grease monkey named Ross McGuire. Mallory always made it clear that she never understood what Kim saw in him, other than it was the boy who took her virginity. But that's another story.

Tonight, Kim had let Mallory talk her into joining the rest of the world --- where tonight everyone would be ringing in the New Year. Here, the entire town of Stillwater would be attending the Congressman's New Year's Eve party at Black Moon Manor. It was the perfect opportunity to find the new love of her life.

"Wear red or nothing at all," Mallory said. "This is your first night out since you cut that 180 pound tumor out of your life. You need to look young and vibrant and energetic."

"I can't wear this. This looks like something a drag queen would wear in a Madonna video." She ran her hands through her thick black hair, piling it on top her head then glanced at Zeus. The Doberman lifted his eyes and huffed. Kim laughed, receiving the message loud and clear.

Mallory continued. "If I know Dr. Whitman, that dress will really turn him on."

"I'm not interested in turning him on." Kim really didn't want to meet this man, but Mallory was always pushing her into uncomfortable situations.

Kim had known Mallory a few years now. She was ten years older, but not nearly as mature. Mallory had lived next door ever since Kim moved into the gated townhome community, and in that time had become, by default or by convenience, her best friend. In her heart, she wanted to describe their friendship as Lucy and Ethel. But it was Mallory, not her, who was the adventurous red head. By Kim's standards, Mallory was a wild, free-spirited force of nature who, inexplicably, was a magnet for both men and money. Now Mallory was introducing her to one of those men. *Why couldn't it have been the money?* Kim thought, then added, "Besides, he's not a doctor... he's a head shrink."

"What do you think a shrink is?" Mallory flipped through a small closet crammed full of clothes, belts, shoes, hats, scarves and who knows what else. In the clutter, she found a skimpy royal blue dress and pulled it off the hanger. "Besides, you're missing the point. The man's crazy in love with you."

Kim shook her head. "He's never even met me."

"But I've told him all about you. He's crazy in love with you. There's no other way to describe it."

"Well, he's going to think I charge by the hour if I show up at the party wearing this dress." She turned her back to the mirror and reached for the zipper. "I want to wear that navy blue skirt and matching jacket. The one with the little white buttons."

Mallory made a disgusted face and pretended to gag. "You can't wear that. I already told you, you look depressing in dark colors."

"It's understated. Muted," Kim said. "And besides, it's how I feel." She unzipped the gown, letting it fall to the floor. "I really don't want to go. I'm not into head shrinks with obsessive personalities."

A knock on the door downstairs interrupted the girls and the Doberman leapt to his feet, barking. Mallory turned her head as a deep voice echoed through the townhome.

"Ladies, time is of the essence. We're in a fantastic hurry."

It was Mallory's date, a tall, rather well-fed chap dressed in a tuxedo. He was considerably older than either Mallory or Kim, with graying temples and a carefully trimmed salt-and-pepper beard and mustache. People often compared him to Sean Connery, and Mallory loved that about him.

Zeus barked excitedly and scrambled down the spiral staircase.

"It's Addison," Mallory said under her breath. "And damn it, he's early."

Kim glanced at her watch. It was a quarter after eight. Actually, he was almost forty-five minutes late, she thought. Mallory had been dating Addison for as long as Kim had known her - just not exclusively.

Mallory often described him as necessary, like going to the dentist. It's not something you enjoy doing, but it's something you have to do if you want to look your best. And Addison did make Mallory look good; he bought her clothing and jewelry. A solid twenty years older, he was wealthy, owning a successful insurance business and properties throughout Stillwater. He was nice though, and sometimes Kim felt bad for the way Mallory treated him.

As Zeus tripped over his feet to welcome him inside, Mallory leaned over the banister at the edge of the loft and waved.

"We're not dressed yet, Pudd'n Toes," she called to him. "Give us just a minute."

Addison stepped into the living room, glancing at the Doberman and then up at her.

"Now, Mallory, I must insist..." He placed his hands on his hips and leaned forward, looking up at her. "It's after eight, and you know dilatory entrances are one of my issues."

"Oh, baby... Take a Valium," she yelled back at him. "And make yourself comfortable." Zeus watched Addison's every move with intense interest, his large brown eyes growing as the man paced the living room.

"Where's the shrink?" Kim joined Mallory at the banister and leaned over the railing, trying to see past Addison and out the door. But he blocked her view. "I thought you were both meeting us here."

"We're rendezvousing with Dr. Whitman at the benefit precisely at nine o'clock." His voice was stern and authoritative, and he had no intention of being late. "Dr. Whitman stated he received a call from a patient who was abnormally anxious of the Y2K bug," he added.

"I can't believe this." Kim pulled away and sat on the bed. Mallory turned and followed.

"It's okay. The Y2K is an urban myth." She sat down on the bed beside her. "Your computer will be fine."

"That's not what I'm talking about." Kim put her face in her hands. "This is my first date in over four years and I'm already getting ditched."

Mallory stood up, grabbed an arm and pulled her back to her feet. "He's waiting for you at the party, okay?"

"I'm not going." Kim picked up the red gown, returning it to a hanger in the cramped closet. There was barely room for it, but it didn't matter. Mallory immediately grabbed the gown and handed it back to her.

"Yes. You are. Now quit whining."

"The guy sounds old," Kim continued, pleading her point. "I'm not into old guys like you are."

"He's not old, he's seasoned." Mallory thrust the gown in her face. Kim hesitantly took the dress as Mallory continued. "And he has money. And he's a doctor."

Kim looked at the gaudy red dress clutched in her hands, and resigned to her fate.

"He's a shrink," she said.

Thirty minutes later Kim and Mallory appeared at the top of the spiral staircase and posed like fashion models on the steps. Mallory swayed her hips and shoulders, her body squeezed into a tight, short-skirted, royal blue slip of a dress. Her eyes were outlined in dark mascara, her lips in scarlet, and her silky red hair pinned-up and wrapped around her head like a crown. She waved to Addison and blew him a kiss.

Kim, dressed in the red gown with leopard print breasts, her hair piled into a mass of black curls atop her head, stretched her arms and mimicked an exaggerated pose from a fashion magazine.

"Well, Addison," Mallory said in a husky voice. "Get a load of us."

"Were we worth the wait?" Kim blushed, a little embarrassed. Addison looked up at them. He flashed a vague smile, stepped back, then shook his head.

"Frankly, no." He took Mallory's coat from the entry hall closet and moved toward the front door. His arm bumped the keys hanging on a hook and they dropped to the floor with a rattling clink. Addison bent over to pick them up as he glanced at his wrist watch. "We should've departed an hour ago."

"But doesn't Kim look delicious?" Mallory insisted, as if completely oblivious to his bad mood. She stretched her arms outward to present her creation to the awaiting public. "I picked out the gown myself."

"Yes. Simply divine." Agitation grew in his voice. "I'm sure she'll have the attention of every man in attendance. Now, I must insist. We're in a fantastic hurry." After returning the keys to the hook on the wall, he held up the coat and opened the door.

Mallory hesitated.

"Every man?" Her eyebrows narrowed. "You really think Kim looks that hot?"

"She's positively breathtaking. Stunning. Exquisite." The coat still in his arms, he pointed to his watch. "Now, it's almost nine o'clock..."

Mallory paid no attention. She was studying Kim with her arms crossed.

Kim took a quick breath of utter astonishment. "What's wrong now?"

"I'm sorry Kimberly, but you just can't leave the house wearing that outfit." Mallory shook her head, placing her hands on her hips. "You look like a drag queen in a Madonna video."

"You want me to change? We don't have time."

"Girls please!" Addison flailed his arms. He dropped the coat.

"I know! I know," Mallory said, pushing Kim back upstairs. "We're in a fantastic hurry."

* * * * * * *

Next door, inside Kim's dark townhome, the front door unlocked and creaked open.

A man stepped into the living room, the porch light bright behind him. He shut the door, locked it, then took a flashlight from his jacket. The long, narrow beam pierced the blackness as he stepped through the townhome.

The kitchen was obviously a mess. Even in the

limited light he could see the grime from the garbage disposal that covered the sink and cabinets; soggy towels laid across the floor.

The man moved from the kitchen and aimed the light back toward the living room, shining it on the wrought-iron staircase spiraling up to a bedroom loft. Cautiously, he stepped upstairs.

Clothing was scattered on the floor and from the radio beside the bed came a quiet static. The man moved to the bed, setting down the flashlight. He glanced out the sloping skylight above it. He was alone, engulfed in darkness.

Quickly he turned, grasped the bed sheets and pulled them to his face, inhaling deeply. Shutting his eyes, he sighed.

From the bedroom window, he watched Kim and Mallory leave for the night, alone.

2
New Year's Evil

Two hours late and without their escorts, Mallory, dressed in the red designer gown with leopard print breasts, and Kim, dressed in a conservative navy skirt and matching jacket, her face intelligently framed with reading glasses, made their way through the wrought iron security gates and entered Black Moon Manor, the Congressman's estate. Gliding up the sweeping stone steps leading to a grand front entrance, they smiled at the valets and held out their hands to the attendants at the front door.

"I can't believe Addison left us." Kim handed her wrap to an attendant. "I told you we shouldn't have changed clothes again."

"Pipe down, darling," Mallory answered her rather flatly. "It's fashionable to be late."

"Where's the shrink?" Kim couldn't believe the number of people around them, getting out of cars and making their way inside. The muffled beat of music pounded from the mansion ahead. It was almost too much.

Mallory took Kim's hand and pulled her forward. "The dashing Dr. Whitman is probably inside some- where, pouring you a drink."

They entered the mansion, stepping into a brilliant foyer decorated with ferns and statues. The floor was black marble and Kim could actually see her reflection beneath her feet. She couldn't believe she let Mallory talk her into leaving her contacts at home and wearing those stupid glasses.

She started to say something when she noticed Mallory focused intently on the room, smirking, apparently satisfied with what she saw. Leaning toward her ear, Mallory took her by the arm and whispered.

"Dogs - they're all dogs." Her voice dripped with judgment. "If someone brought a quail inside, I bet every woman in this room would stand up and point."

"You're awful..." Kim looked around to see if anyone had overheard them.

The New Year's Eve party was a gala event. In the glitter of the fashionably dressed crowd, Kim spotted many familiar faces - all famous: Sports heroes. Newscasters. Politicians. Television stars. And the host, Congressman William Dietz, was at the center of it all.

Kim judged him to be in his late thirties, if not forty, but that assessment was based purely on media reports and his career position. Physically, he looked to be in his mid-thirties. His hair was thinning ever so slightly above his forehead, and it gave him an air of sincerity and down-to-earth ruggedness. His body leaned toward the stocky side, despite media buzz that he was an ardent jogger. And he had an infamous claim to fame.

Twenty-five years ago, his older, high school brother was murdered in the dark lake just beyond the estate. The popular senior on the varsity wrestling team had snuck away to go skinny dipping with a freshman girl. His body was found floating, decimated, missing his right eye. Her body was still missing to this day. And, it was a mystery that had never been solved. Locals claimed a gator attacked the kids. It was the only explanation that made sense. Of course, there were whispers of murder.

Even Kim and Mallory knew of this legend, but it wasn't on the forefront of their minds this once-in-a-lifetime New Year's Eve. They simply wanted to thank him for extending the invitation. Unfortunately, by the time they made their way across the room to talk to him, Congressman Dietz was surrounded by hordes of people.

With no alternative, the girls walked away. Mallory announced she was finding Addison and coaxing him onto the dance floor. Kim tried to protest as he was still clearly nowhere to be found.

As Mallory wandered away, Kim accepted a glass of wine from a passing waiter. She wondered what had happened to her date. The shrink wasn't here, she was pretty sure of that. And it only proved that she didn't belong here either.

At least holding a glass of wine would make her look like she belonged. So much had already happened this evening, she thought. And it was as if each incident was screaming at her to just go home and forget the whole night.

She was lost in thought when a waiter nudged her again, slipping a folded note into her hand.

"A gentleman asked that I give this to you."

Kim thanked him and unfolded the paper. A message had been scribbled on it: *"If you forget me, there's something I want you to know."* She shook her head.

"Ross," she sighed. Three weeks, four days, and eighteen hours. Now he was crawling back to her. She looked back at the waiter. "Who gave this to you?"

"He didn't leave a name, ma'am."

"Can you point him out?" She scanned the crowded room and studied all the people laughing and drinking. She expected to see him standing in the corner, smiling at her. But he wasn't among them. The waiter turned his head.

"I don't see him," he said.

"What'd he look like? Was he tall, swimmer's build, early twenties, with short black hair?"

"I'm sorry. I just wasn't paying attention. I was serving drinks and he came up behind me. I didn't really get a good look..."

Searching the room, her eyes studied each guest. She moved slowly through the crowd, then turned focusing on every face. She couldn't take her mind off the note: *"If you forget me, there's something I want you to know."* She knew precisely what it meant. He was here. Somewhere, Ross was here. But had he come back for her? Distracted, she walked right into the Congressman. SMACK! His hand jerked backwards, spilling wine down the front of his tuxedo. Surprised, Kim stepped back.

"I'm so sorry." Her heart stopped and she nearly dropped the glass.

"Don't worry about it... the tux is rented." He laughed, glancing at the mess she made. Kim took her napkin and gently dabbed at the wine dripping down the front of his jacket.

"I can't believe I just did that."

"You're Kimberly Bradford, aren't you?" he asked. Kim stopped dabbing and looked up into his face. He was smiling at her. "You're friends with Addison Gaynor."

She opened her mouth slightly, searching for the words. "You're... you're not a shrink, are you?"

"No. I'm William Dietz, your friendly neighborhood Congressman." His grin widened. "Mr. Gaynor told me of your recent and unfortunate separation. He also told me that you're attending my little party unaccompanied."

"Really?" Kim thought that was odd. She pushed the reading glasses up further on her nose. "I just don't know where my date is."

"Well, whether he turns up or not, I hope you'll save a dance for me." The Congressman took her hand in his.

"Of course. It would be my pleasure." She

forced a thin smile. The mob of people who had
followed and surrounded the Congressman all
evening long returned, pushing Kim out of the way.
But despite the swarming commotion, he never took
his eyes off her.

"I'll be looking for you later." He kissed the back
of her hand, then turned, slipping between two small
groups of people loitering by the buffet and holding
little plates of hors d'oeuvres. A moment later he was
gone, swallowed by the crowd.

Kim set down her empty wine glass and raised
a hand to her flushed face.

Ten minutes later, she found Mallory in the
powder room, engrossed with her image in the
mirror, reapplying a heavy coat of lipstick. Kim
approached her, holding up the note.

"I've got news," she said, excitement creeping
into her voice. "Look what the waiter handed me."

Mallory didn't even acknowledge her. Kim
continued anyway.

"Ross is here. He wrote this note." She paused
looking around the lavatory. "I wouldn't be surprised if
he's hiding in here somewhere, spying on us right
now!" Paranoid, Kim turned to the water closet
behind them. Mallory glanced at the note, but still
showed little interest.

"There's a blonde here with breasts out to
there." Mallory held her arms out in front of her body
to describe an exaggerated size of her own breasts
in the leopard print material. "She thinks she's got
every guy here drooling but I don't think anybody
really believes that boobs just accidentally pop out at

inappropriate moments. Like they need to come up for air or something..."

"Mal, listen to me. Ross is here. He sent me a note. Do you know what this means?"

"I think she's trying to start a music career or something," Mallory said, once again puckering at her image in the mirror. "But she'd better watch herself. I may just take her out right here in front of everybody, boobs and all!"

"Mal, I'm having a crisis. Are you even listening to me?" Kim shoved the note in her face. Mallory put down the lipstick.

"No, I'm not listening. If I don't ever hear Ross' name again, it will still be too soon!" She twisted shut the tube of lipstick, then grabbed the note. She glanced over it. "He didn't even sign this. How do you know this is from Ross?"

The lavatory door opened, interrupting the girls. Making a grand entrance, the well-endowed blonde walked inside the powder room. Mallory glared at her. The blonde glared back and then stepped into the water closet, shutting the door.

"She thinks she's so hot," Mallory grumbled. "Slutty Miss Stillwater 1995."

Kim looked back at the note. "I can't believe Ross has finally come back..."

Outside the powder room, Kim and Mallory wandered toward the ballroom. Men and women were dancing around them as a live band played "Mambo No. 5."

Kim glanced at the black tie crowd then sighed.

She had to yell at Mallory to be heard over the rhythmic beat of the song. "Where's Addison?"

"I haven't seen him all evening." Mallory focused on the crowd.

Kim glanced at the band. "Maybe he went home with the shrink."

"They're both here, somewhere," Mallory yelled.

"I just want to find Ross."

"You're making too much of this!"

"He's come back to me. Come on, help me find him." Kim tugged on Mallory's arm, trying to lead her away from the dance floor. Mallory resisted and drew back her arm.

"He was your high school boyfriend," she said. "High school is over. Let him go."

"We're soul mates," she insisted. "This note is proof that he's realized that too." Kim suddenly stopped walking, her exit blocked by a man.

Tall and athletic, he approached the girls.

"Prospero Año Nuevo," he said with a heavy Cuban accent, his voice deep. "You would like dance?" He was dark and Hispanic with smoldering good looks and a boyish charm. His white tuxedo shirt and black pants strained to contain a muscle-beach-boy body that had brought his major league career strength, speed and steroid speculation. He seemed entranced with Mallory, staring intently into her eyes.

"Have we met?" Mallory flashed him a wicked grin as she stroked her bottom lip with her index finger.

"I'm The Gunz," he said to her. "We should

dance?"

Mallory laughed, batting her eyes. Kim nudged her, trying to get her attention.

"Mal, I'm in crisis mode and you're flirting with a stranger!" Kim said. Clearly, Mallory didn't hear a word. She was focused on the athlete in front of them.

"You look familiar..." Mallory cocked her head and put her index finger to her lip as if his name was on the tip of her tongue. "Are you famous?"

The man smiled broadly. He only got better looking.

"I'm Antonio Gonzales, Second Baseman..." He spoke as if he hoped to elicit a response of recognition, but Mallory stared blankly at him. Seemingly, taken off guard, he stumbled to explain himself. "The New York Yankee's. We just swept Atlanta in the World Series..."

Mallory stared wide-eyed. She didn't blink. He continued.

"I was on the cover of Sports Illustrated."

Mallory looked as perplexed as ever; it meant nothing to her. Kim intervened, placing a hand on Mallory's shoulder.

"Maybe if you had been on the cover of Forbes," she suggested. Mallory gently pushed her aside and smiled at the man.

"So, second baseman..." Mallory's eyes sparkled, her left hand lightly grazing his massive right biceps barely constrained in its shirt sleeve. "You play football."

"Baseball," he corrected.

Mallory laughed again, excited. She then locked her arm in his, leading him to the dance floor.

Shaking her head in disbelief, Kim watched the two disappear, then once again glanced at the note in her hands.

"If you forget me, there's something I want you to know" was all it said. This was proof, she thought. And she moved through the crowd, searching for the waiter who handed it to her, or possibly Ross himself.

When she ran into Addison, he looked frantic and upset.

"Why, Addison," she exclaimed. "Where have you been?"

Addison took her hands in his. "Kimberly, have you seen Mallory?"

"Yes," Kim said slowly, clutching the note, then asked again. "Where have you been all evening?"

On the dance floor, Mallory and The Gunz held each other close and tightly rocked together as the band began a slow song.

"I never meet lady like you," he said to her. She smiled devilishly and nodded.

"And you never will." She held his hard, sun-darkened face between her soft hands and kissed him, drawing the breath from his body. Then finally she gasped and pulled her head away. "Would you believe I'm still innocent?"

"Como una Virgen..." His hands moved on her back, kneading the tender flesh in an outpour of desire that was beyond either's ability to control. His hand slid lower to cup the firm, round swell of her hip.

"Do you want me..." Mallory was panting now. She had to concentrate on each word to speak, "...as badly as I want you?"

"¡Ay, caramba!" The Gunz bent her back in his arms and looked her squarely eye to eye. He groaned.

Suddenly, a hand forced its way between the two straining bodies. It was Addison Gaynor, prying them apart. Mallory's eyes enlarged.

"Why, Pudd'n Toes - I was just looking for you," she said quickly, taking her hands from the ball player's grasp.

Grabbing Mallory by the arm, Addison yanked her off the dance floor.

Kim followed Mallory and Addison as they pushed their way through the crowd. Addison was lecturing, on the verge of hyperventilating.

"Mallory Astin, this is scandalous. Just scandalous!" He waved his arms as his voice rose. "What in the name of all that is good has come over you? And wasn't Kim wearing that dress earlier?"

Mallory didn't seem to be listening. Turning her head, she glanced at The Gunz, who was still standing on the dance floor. She winked at him. A moment later, they had disappeared around the corner and down the hall.

Walking past the corner too, Kim hesitated, feeling his presence. Ross was here. Watching her. She could feel his breath like a firm, invisible grip. Turning her head, she saw no one familiar in the crowd. *Was it just her imagination?*

Stepping into the entrance way, Kim ran after Mallory and Addison. His voice echoed in the marble hallway and carried over the music. "Just scandalous," he said again. "Scandalous!"

Before midnight, Kim accepted a dance with the Congressman. She was graceful and light on her feet. But there was an awkward distance between them.

Mallory had found The Gunz on the dance floor. Their bodies meshed together so completely they could have been one person. Kim watched them, then smiled as Addison once again pried them apart and yanked Mallory from the ballroom.

The countdown began ten seconds to midnight. Everyone on the dance floor stopped. Laughing and toasting, their voices counted down together, like one loud amplifier.

Ten... Nine... Eight...

Kim smiled at the Congressman. Around them, waiters were handing out glasses of champagne. He took two and handed one flûte to Kimberly, then they locked their arms together and joined in the countdown.

Seven... Six... Five...

Kim's eyes searched the ocean of people for Mallory. She was standing beside Addison as he was counting loudly with the crowd. Mallory noticed the well-endowed blonde from the powder room and shot her a dirty look. The blonde stuck out her tongue.

Kim wasn't paying any attention. It was the end of the nineteen-nineties, and the end of the Twentieth

Century. And she couldn't believe she was spending the New Year's Eve of a Lifetime at the most exciting party in town, locked arm in arm with one of the most charming, celebrated bachelors she'd ever met. Their eyes locked with the final seconds. Still she wondered where Ross was.

Four... Three... Two...

"ONE!" Kim screamed just as the Congressman wrapped an arm around her and brought her toward him. With one swift movement, he removed the reading glasses from her face and kissed her. When their lips parted, he beamed and yelled, "Happy New Year!"

She could barely hear him over the cheering and screaming. Balloons fell from the ceiling as confetti floated in the air. The music was blaring. And Kim noticed she had once again spilled her champagne down the front of his tuxedo. He shrugged it off and brought her close to him, tightly squeezing her.

Kim turned so that her cheek rested on the Congressman's shoulder. They slow danced amid the celebration around them, and she gripped his right hand in hers.

Still, her eyes wandered the room. She thought about the shrink and wondered what happened to him. *Had he really stood her up?* Then she thought about Ross, and if he was here somewhere, lost in the crowd, watching her. Pushing the thought further from her mind, she wrapped an arm tighter around the Congressman's waist.

There was a throbbing pang of alarm somewhere deep in her temples. More than just a dull headache. She could feel it. Something was about to happen.

* * * * * * *

From the shadows of the ballroom, a man blended with the crowd and watched Kim and the Congressman hold each other, slowly rocking back and forth. He imagined what they were talking about. He could see them whispering into each other's ear.

Stepping away from the pillars in the corners, he moved across the dance floor, hidden among bodies, unseen and unnoticed. Moving into the hallway, he slipped up the large carpeted staircase and disappeared into a room upstairs.

"If you forget me," he said. "There's something I want you to know."

3
Dead Man's Time

Saturday, January 1, 2000
2:03 AM

Twenty miles north of Tampa, a semi truck pulled into the parking lot at the Flying J Truck Stop, grumbling loudly as it rolled past the frail phone booth. A teenage girl, no more than sixteen, came out of the store carrying a Big Gulp in one hand and a suit case in another. She'd been crying.

Behind her, a Chevy pick-up carrying an angry boyfriend skidded out of the parking lot and onto the street. Its tires screeched as he sped away. Through teary eyes, she watched him leave.

Out the corner of her eye, she noticed the big semi truck pull around and park. Brakes squealed as steam released above the tires. It blocked her view of the storefront and engulfed her in deep shadows. Standing at the phone booth, the crying teenager fished a quarter out of her pocket and deposited it into the coin slot. She dialed. The phone rang.

That's when she noticed it: A sticky, reddish-brown gunk on the pay phone, more reddish-brown splatters on the plexi-glass. She touched the glass, removing a spec of crust.

The receiver to her ear, she listened to it ring again. Her father answered.

"Brianna, is that you?" came his overjoyed voice through the phone. *"Happy New Year, baby... Are you okay?"*

"Daddy..." She looked around. There was a puddle of the reddish-brown stuff at her feet, and a trail winding through the pavement in the parking lot.

"Daddy..." Her voice trembled. "I think something's happened..."

* * * * * * *

Kim and Mallory made it home after two that morning. Zeus was waiting for them and Kim could see his head staring impatiently out the front bay window in Mallory's townhome as they pulled up. Mallory was still begging for details about Kim's time with the Congressman as Zeus greeted them with leaps and bounds, wagging his stubby tail. Mallory screamed at him for jumping on her. Kim hugged him and walked him next door to their home.

Once the Doberman was fed, walked and laying securely at her feet, she collapsed in her grandfather's old recliner and wrapped herself in the hand-stitched quilt her grandmother had made.

Burrowed into the quilt as if she could stave off the cold dread stealing over her, she waited for Ross. To pass the time she found an old scrapbook and thumbed through the pages. Between its covers were all the love letters he had ever written to her.

She lifted one handwritten poem from the book. A poem she'd read for the gazillionth time. Sighing, she read it once again.

> *"Oh, Love rips the heart in pieces,*
> *When distance fills the empty creases*
> *Of time*
> *And days become long stretches*
> *Of pain and wretches*
> *Of torment*
> *When our love ceases.*
>
> *"So take what little comfort and solace*
> *To atone*
> *In knowing that you are not alone,*
> *For every tear that you have shed*
> *My own heart has wept and bled."*

Ross wrote that, and it made Kim smile.

Turning, she read the note she'd received at the New Year's Eve Party again. *"If you forget me, there's something I want you to know."* Her eyes tearing, she placed it on a blank page. It was now three weeks, five days and 23 hours.

"Oh, Ross," she said quietly, impatiently. *Where was he? Would he call? Or would he just show up at her door step?* She imagined the door bursting open and Ross stepping inside. He would come to her, pick her up in his arms, then carry her upstairs to their bed.

Over the last three weeks, she had considered time and again just dropping by his job at Eddy's Garage downtown. But she didn't want to make the first move. She didn't want to look desperate. So she waited. Kim knew sooner or later, Ross would contact her.

By two-thirty, she found the remote and turned on the television. She flipped aimlessly from channel to channel until finding an "I Love Lucy" rerun.

Shifting comfortably in the recliner, she laughed. Lucy read a murder mystery and now she thought Ricky was trying to do her in. She'd seen this episode a hundred times, and it made her miss being a little girl who would climb in her Grampa's lap when he was trying to read the newspaper. With no other option, he would turn on reruns of "I Love Lucy" and she would curl up beside him, and they would laugh and laugh.

Zeus lifted his head, cocking it to one side, and watched her. Rising to his feet, he climbed into her lap. Kim squealed and pushed him down, yelling that he was too big to climb into the chair with her.

By three, she turned off the TV plunging the room in darkness. She stared at the phone, willing him to call. At some point, she dozed into a light, restless sleep.

When she woke again, Kim felt cold and alone. Slipping out from under the heavy quilt, she moved toward the bay window, opened the drapes and stared outside. The moon had long since vanished and the sky was black and forbidding; an angry January wind howled and pressed violently against the glass. She paid no attention to it as her mind wandered, and her eyes followed the room, coming to Ross' smiling face in the framed photographs hanging on the wall. The scrapbook with ripped notebook pages of handwritten love letters lay on the chair.

Three weeks, six days and four hours. Where was he?

"I think something's happened..." she said.

* * * * * * *

Saturday, January 1, 2000
10:35 AM

Black Moon Manor was quietly lit with morning sunlight streaming in through the windows, and the Congressman's bedroom, with an eastern exposure, was especially bright making sleep impossible. A mass of blonde curls with a little head poked up from under the covers and groaned. *Why hadn't they drawn the drapery last night? Didn't he have people*

JC Gatlin

who saw to those kinds of details, she thought.

Stretching an arm, she reached for the Congressman, but found the sheets empty and cold beside her. The blonde sat up and groggily forced one eye open. She was alone in bed. Unsnapping the handcuffs dangling around her right wrist, she wrapped a sheet around her naked body and slipped out the room.

"Warren, honey?" she called out in the hallway. There was no answer; the large house was silent. The Congressman had given his staff the day off for tending last night's New Year's Eve party and now the house seemed deathly still.

She walked to the edge of the staircase and leaned over the banister. She tried to remember his name. *Was it Warren or Willie or Webster?*

"Winchester? Are you hiding again?"

There was no answer. She tiptoed downstairs. The large rooms, the banquet hall and the dining room were all a mess, littered from the enormous amount of people now gone. She entered the kitchen.

Long, narrow and stainless steel, it looked even worse than the banquet hall. Jell-O and eggs were splattered along the countertops. Chicken and ham sat spoiling in the sink. Melted ice cream and ketchup, mustard and olives were left on the island beside an overturned carton of milk. Shelves from inside the refrigerator lay scattered on the countertops and across the floor. The girl ran her hands through her long blonde mane and laughed.

"Looks like a hurricane blew through this place,"

she said and wondered if there was anything left for breakfast. Or at least a hangover.

She opened the refrigerator and peered inside, then froze. The sheet wrapped around her body fell to her ankles, as her hands rose to her mouth. She screamed.

Congressman William Dietz was staring back at her from inside the refrigerator, folded and stuffed like a frozen rag doll. Dark brownish-red blood stained his head, matting his hair to his skull and leaving long streaks down his face. Thin layers of ice flaked on his pale cheeks and in his eyelashes. His left eye, wide open in terror, was vacant. His right eye was gone, leaving a bloody brown crater where his eye socket had been.

The blonde stepped back, gasping for breath. She clutched her hands over her breasts and tried to calm herself. She was trying to think. What should she do? She stumbled to the table and clutched a chair to help her stand. *Who should she call?*

She inhaled deeply, remembering the acting exercises she learned in class to relieve anxiety. She closed her eyes then counted backwards from ten.

Nine... Eight... Seven... Six...

Okay, she decided. I'm calm. Straightening her back, she regained her composure. First, she shut the refrigerator, then looked for a phone. There was one on the wall at the end of the counter.

She picked up the receiver and dialed "0."

"Operator, this is an emergency," she said quickly. "I need the number for People Magazine."

JC Gatlin

A week later...

JC Gatlin

4
A Cold Day for Murder

Monday, January 10, 2000
7:35 AM

"INVESTIGATION CONTINUES OF MURDERED CONGRESSMAN, EX-MISS STILLWATER QUESTIONED BY POLICE" screamed the headline. Kim couldn't believe it, picking up the morning paper from her doorstep.

Slamming the front door, she unfolded it and scanned the article. It had been a week since the body was found and it still shocked her. Police had questioned her a couple of days ago. They had stopped by the old folk's home where she was visiting her grandfather, and she told them everything she knew. *Everything* except for the handwritten note she'd received.

Kim knew the love poem was not connected to the murder, and even though Ross still hadn't called her or come home, he was out there. It was just a matter of time before he came for her. And she wished that she knew where he was.

Zeus' barking distracted her, and she put the newspaper down beside her school books on the kitchen table. The Doberman was growling at the overalls and work boots sprawled out on the linoleum floor, the man's upper-half hidden under the sink. The garbage disposal was acting up again, and the landlord swore he'd fix it this time.

"Zeus!" she yelled. Rushing to the sink she grabbed the dog by the collar. "I'm so sorry! How's the faucet?"

"What?" his voice was muffled under the sink. He strained to be heard over the barking.

"I said, 'How's the faucet?'"

"Missy, you're a fine tenant." He flipped out from under the sink and held a ratchet in his right hand. Like all landlords, he was simultaneously crotchety yet a knowledgeable southern gentleman, in his late sixties and the product of another era. Kim had known him for several years now and, in all that time, had never seen him wear anything but the same ole blue jean overalls and weathered straw hat. He picked the hat up off the kitchen floor and placed it on top his bald head as he continued his lecture. "But the good Lord knows I'm seriously considering adding a 'No-Pets Clause' to your lease."

Zeus barked again and he cringed. Kim gripped the collar to hold back the dog.

"I'm sorry. I gotta get to class, but I'll take Zeus with me." She dragged the dog backwards across the linoleum as he let loose a spasm of barks, yelps and a copious string of slobber.

"What?" The landlord cupped a hand to his ear as if he couldn't hear a thing over Zeus' tantrum.

"I gotta go to class!" With one hand gripping the leash and holding back her growling dog, Kim grabbed her text books from the kitchen table. She left the newspaper behind.

"I can't hear you over the dog!" he yelled again. And again, Kim apologized, dragging Zeus out of the kitchen.

"Just consider this payback for the dress your garbage disposal ruined on New Year's Eve," she said to him. "That cost me a hundred fifty dollars."

The landlord ignored her. "I'm serious about the No-Pets Clause."

Zeus growled again. Kim tugged on his collar, pulling him to the front door. With books in hand, she and Zeus were outside and walking across the lawn toward the sidewalk leading to the gated entrance.

The Doberman, sighing, finally complied with her direction, until he saw a Pekingese named Rosie that lived in the townhome across the street. Mrs. Roundtree was walking the little dog, and Zeus immediately scrambled in that direction. Kim yanked hard on the leash, causing Zeus to double back.

"Come on," Kim said to him through clenched teeth, dragging the dog across the grass. Zeus locked down, focused on the Pekingese and barked. Little Rosie stopped, looked in his direction, and yelped back. Now Zeus growled, and Kim tugged harder on the leash.

"Would. You. Come. On." Kim forced the words out her mouth, somewhere between growling herself and yelling, all the while hoping the thin leather leash didn't snap.

Ultimately, her will being stronger, Kim won the tug of war and Zeus turned and followed her to the sidewalk. They exited the gate and walked toward downtown Stillwater, headed to the University.

* * * * * * *

For reasons known only to her, Kim often took the long way to the University.

Today was no different and she walked Zeus along the out-of-way, winding, busy Morris Munger Road. She could have cut through downtown and made it to class in just under twenty minutes. But she rarely took that route anymore, opting instead to add a good half hour to her trip. She had adopted this custom since her last night with Ross. And every time she made her way down Morris Munger Road, she stepped deliberately along the shoulder, staring down at her feet, staring intently at the viney stink weeds, dandelions and occasional Coke bottle.

As the cars whooshed past, she would hesitate at the same point on the street. Stop here every single time.

The dilapidated sign advertising a cow pasture

that was now commercial land for sale was a significant landmark known only to her. It stood near the curb, where Morris Munger curved and a long abandoned wooden fruit stand was rotting on the other side. Many times over the past five weeks, Kim had searched the ground there, picking through the tall grass sprouting around the sign posts and within the drainage grate along the curve. Sometimes, she would cross the street and search the ground around the fruit stand.

That real estate sign and lonely fruit stand were the only witnesses to that night Ross left her standing on the gravel shoulder.

Today, she held her books tightly in one arm and tugged on Zeus' leash with the other, holding him back as she waited for a break in the traffic. When the street was empty, and she had looked for cars coming from either direction, Kim and Zeus jumped out to the center of the road. There, she knelt down by yellow painted dash marks and searched the hot concrete, ran a hand over the grains of gravel like a miner sifting for gold.

Zeus stared at her, his head cocked.

A brown and tan station wagon screamed past them, blaring its horn. It blew Kim's hair and she dropped her books. Papers scattered across the pavement as Zeus barked at the car.

Collecting her books, Kim scooped them up and dragged Zeus back to the shoulder of the road. She would continue her search later.

Morris Munger Road ran west of downtown Stillwater toward the University campus. It cut through several blocks of two- and three-story homes built along brick-paved streets. These had once been the residences of Stillwater's exclusive, upper class.

Today, the neighborhood was student housing featuring front porches littered with bikes and old furniture, rap music blaring from open dormer windows, and humming window-unit air conditioners. Most of these old houses were in desperate need of a fresh coat of paint, a handyman, and some yard work. Those in best condition proudly displayed Greek letters beneath the eaves and college flags strung along upper-story banister railings.

Two boys hung over the railing of one of the dormitory homes and waved at Kim as she walked Zeus along the sidewalks toward winding paths cutting across the campus. Zeus saw the boys and tugged on his leash to cross the street toward them, but Kim tugged back, leading him toward the University.

The campus was a ten-acre forested park with twisting sidewalks that meandered past a 100-year old brick library and a state-of-art sports facility with sprawling athletic fields. The faculty parking lot ran behind the sports center, and Kim found a city bus stop and pay phone. There, she dialed Mallory.

"I need you to pick up Zeus and take him back to your place."

"Sure," Mallory's voice crackled through the receiver on the sticky handset of the campus pay phone. *"I'll be right there."*

And all Kim could do now was wait.

It was the first day back after winter break and

the start of a new semester, which meant the campus was more crowded and chaotic than usual. And Kimberly bringing her Doberman only added to the commotion. Everyone wanted to pet him and Zeus adored the attention.

Setting her books down beside her on the park bench, Kim waited in the university parking lot for Mallory to arrive. When her white Mazda Miata pulled up to the curb, Zeus barked and jumped. Holding the leash, she got up from the park bench and made her way to Mallory's car. Zeus greeted her as she opened the driver's side door.

"Thanks for taking him this afternoon." Kim pet Zeus on the head as he licked her cheek. "With the landlord fixing the sink and this crazy animal acting like —"

"I know. I know. What would you do without me?" Mallory grabbed her keys and tossed them into her purse. Leaning down, she greeted Zeus and patted him on top the head. Finally turning back to Kim, she said, "I've only got a moment. I have to be back at my place by one. If KYGL calls and I don't answer with the *phrase that pays*, I could lose ten thousand dollars!"

"Well, thank you. I owe you one."

Mallory grinned. "Yes, you do."

Kim paused, reading the expression on Mallory's face. "You already have something in mind, don't you?"

"Have dinner with Addison and me tonight." Mallory's face lit up and she gushed. "We're going to celebrate his 50th birthday with dinner and a movie."

"I can't believe you're dating a man old enough to be your father."

"Oh, hush. He's hip," Mallory tempted, leaning against her car. "We're going to see that new Julia Roberts movie."

"Are you kidding? With everything going on?" Kim asked. She realized that she had left her text books and notebook on the park bench. She looked back. A boy was sitting on the bench now. He was thin, with black, wispy hair that fell down over his eyes. She stared at him, judging whether or not to walk back and collect her things. He looked up and their eyes met. She looked away, turning back toward Mallory. "So have they found anything new in the Congressman's murder? I didn't get a chance to read the paper."

"I've been ignoring the whole sordid affair ever since the police questioned me last week. The whole thing's just too horrible for words." Mallory's green eyes enlarged and her lips drew close together. She took hold of Zeus' leash, then changed the subject. "So come with us tonight. It's a birthday party and…" she paused for dramatic effect. "I invited the doctor."

"You mean the shrink with the obsessive personality who stood me up on New Year's." Kim turned away. She looked back at the park bench; the boy was gone. Her books were still there. Everything appeared to be okay. After a moment, she muttered, "No thank you."

"Addison explained what happened. The Doctor got tied up with a patient who was having some kind of panic attack over that whole Y2K computer scare,"

Mallory insisted. "Addison says that the Doctor feels just horrible for standing you up that night, and on New Year's Eve of all nights."

Kim hesitated, thinking about it for a moment. She searched the crowd of students for the boy from the park bench. Giving up, she looked back at Mallory. "How does Addison even know this man anyway?"

"Dr. Whitman's practice is in the same building as Addison's insurance agency," Mallory explained. "And he says that he told Dr. Whitman all about you."

"I don't want to meet him. I'd just prefer to get that whole night as far behind me as possible. I mean with the murder and…"

"But he's sorry and he's so cute. You two would be perfect for each other." Mallory waited for a response, then added, "He's a doctor."

"He's a shrink."

"He makes good money." She paused, then continued slowly. "They're going to meet us at Greico's Italian Fine Cuisine at eight o'clock."

"I have bad memories of that place."

"Because Ross took you there?"

"No, this has nothing to do with Ross," Kim lied. "I'm just busy. The new semester is starting and I have to visit my Grandfather… and Melrose Place is on tonight."

"You're hoping he's going to call you or come by or…"

"This isn't about Ross," Kim insisted. "And even if I did have the time, I wouldn't go out with the shrink again. I don't give second chances."

"He deserves a second chance."

"No," Kim said. She opened the door to Mallory's Mazda and snapped her finger. Zeus jumped inside the little sports car as she continued. "I'm going to be late for class."

With that, she turned her back on Mallory and walked away, returning to the park bench. She collected her books. Everything looked to be in order.

"Fine. You win," Mallory called after her. "Go back inside and sulk. But let me ask you one thing..." she paused, as if waiting for Kim to say something.

"Yes...?" Kim stopped walking but she didn't turn around.

Mallory squinted and she clasped her hands together over her heart. "What'd you think of The Gunz? Isn't he to die for?"

Kim glanced over her shoulder and shot her a wicked smile. She saw Zeus in the front seat of the white Mazda behind her. "Get home so you can answer if KYGL calls you. I hope you win ten thousand dollars."

Turning her head, she walked to the University building, smiling.

* * * * * * *

From the anonymity of the crowded campus, he watched Kimberly talk to the red-headed girl and the

Doberman beside the white Mazda Miata. When she turned, collected her books on the park bench and headed toward the University building, she walked right past him. She didn't even notice him. She never noticed him.

His eyes followed her. She pushed through the entrance doors and disappeared inside. Sighing, he swiped the lock of hair falling down over his eyes and flipped it behind his left ear, then followed her inside.

JC Gatlin

5
Twenty Love Poems
& A Song of Despair

Kim sat in an auditorium-style classroom along with roughly eighty other students. She'd had this professor last semester for literature, and knew what to expect. Trying to stay focused, she listened to his droning, monotone lecture.

"Cyrano de Bergerac is a play written in verse, in rhyming couplets of twelve syllables per line," he was saying in front of the chalkboard, gesturing with his arms.

She made notes in her spiral notebook, but her thoughts dwelled on Ross. She had so many questions, and once again she could feel him watching. Feel his eyes burning holes in the back of her head. Self-consciously, Kim looked up and behind her.

There was a classroom of students around her, but she made eye contact with a boy in the back. It was the student from the park bench, the one with the black, wavy hair that fell into his eyes. He was glaring at her; his eyes bore into her and it gave her chills. The Professor cleared his throat and Kim looked away. She focused on her literature text book and pulled out her binder. She listened as the Professor continued.

"The play is responsible for introducing the word 'panache' into the English language," he was saying. "Cyrano is, in fact, famed for his panache, and the play ends with him saying those words just before his death."

Flipping open the binder, Kim found a small book inside. "*Twenty Love Poems and a Song of Despair*" by Pablo Neruda. She opened the poetry book. The inside front cover was inscribed: "*For my Darling Bonnie. You will always be my angel. Love Daddy.*" An envelope fell out of the book and landed near her ankles. She picked it up and tore it open. An index card slipped out. It too was handwritten in red ink.

"*Greico's Italian Restaurant. I'll be waiting.*" Kim looked around. No one was paying attention. The boy in the back was writing, taking notes. The Professor droned on.

She thought of Addison's 50th birthday celebration there, and wondered if Mallory had slipped the invitation in her book. But that would've been impossible. And Mallory was well aware of her history with Greico's. And with Ross. That was *their* place.

"Ross." Kim nodded to herself and flipped through the poetry book, then tucked the note back inside and closed the binder.

After class, Kim walked to the nursing home approximately six blocks from the University. She entered the building, and an orderly looked up and smiled at her.

"Hi, Miss Bradford," the large woman in aqua-colored scrubs said to her as she wheeled an elderly woman in a wheelchair toward the cafeteria.

"Hi Nurse Carla," Kim returned. "How's he doing?"

"Real good today. He's in his room." Carla paused a moment, fidgeting with the elderly woman in the wheel chair. Once settled, she looked back up at Kim and gave her an exhausted smile. "Child, your grandaddy ate all his peas and carrots, and had a solid bowel movement."

"Thanks for watching out for him," Kim said. "I really appreciate all the extra attention you give him." Nurse Carla smiled and Kim walked past her down the wing. She found the door to her grandfather's room slightly open. Inside, a thin, graying man was sitting in a green fabric recliner, staring out the window.

"Grampa," Kim said, entering the room. "How are you doing today?"

He didn't answer. He stared out the window. She set her books on a tray beside the bed and stepped toward him. Kneeling beside the chair, she took his hand.

"Grampa," she said, leaning over and hugging him. Then, she asked again, "How are you doing today? You flirting with the nurses again?"

He didn't respond. He didn't blink. She wasn't even sure that he was aware that she was there. Still, Kim smiled and lifted a finger to move a strand of hair out of his eyes.

"What'cha looking at?" she asked him, glancing out the window.

A blue jay squawked in a magnolia tree. Mad about something, it took off and soared into the sky. Beyond that, two young boys were running in the courtyard. They were yelling and laughing. Kim wondered if they were someone's grandchildren, or maybe great grandchildren, then looked back at her grandfather. "Where's your glasses," she asked him.

Standing, she walked across the room and found a pair of black-framed bifocals on the nightstand. She returned to him and slipped them on his face. He turned his head slightly, as if suddenly spying something out the window he hadn't noticed before.

"Now isn't that better?" Kim asked, laughing a little. She walked over to the tray beside the bed and picked up her books. She found the poetry book.

"Ross gave me a book today," she continued, picking it up in one hand and grabbing a fold-out chair from the corner. She took it and unfolded it beside him. "You remember Ross don't you?"

Saying nothing, he seemed focused on the children running in the courtyard. Kim watched him a moment, then sat down beside him. "Well, as I told you before, Ross and I have been going through this rough patch but I think we're getting past it now. Life doesn't get any easier. That's what you always say, right?"

He didn't respond. After a moment, she held up the poetry book then opened it on her lap.

"Ross gave me a book today," she said, turning to the first page. "It's called 'Twenty Love Poems and a Song of Despair.' Isn't that romantic?"

Page by page, she read each poem to him. She found one poem of particular interest: "If You Forget Me." Those were the words written on the note she'd received at the New Year's Eve Party. This was the proof: the note and the poetry book were from Ross.

And, he was waiting for her at their restaurant. Sighing, she turned the page.

"Did you ever write Nanna poems when you were young and courting?" she asked him. She watched him a moment, waiting for a response.

There was a yellowing photo of her grandmother in a frame on the nightstand. "Nanna was so beautiful when she was young. She was quite the catch. And I'm sure you were handsome and dashing too. Just like Ross…" Her words trailed off.

As if suddenly noticing someone was beside him, he turned his head, appraising her. "Do you know my daughter?" he asked her in a gravely, tired voice.

Kim smiled. "Of course I do. That's my mother. I'm your granddaughter."

"You look like her," he said "She's about your age, my daughter."

Kim paused a moment, studying him. Then she returned her focus to the book. When she finished reading it to him, she started over and read each poem again.

* * * * * * *

It was dark by the time she walked through downtown, past the University. If it hadn't been so late, she would've walked along Morris Munger Road again, pausing at the curve, searching the ground around the old real estate sign and empty fruit stand.

But Kim decided to take the shorter, direct route home as the night was chilly and a little spooky.

Barely twenty minutes later, she made her way into the gated townhome complex. The invitation in red ink was safely tucked away inside the poetry book, alongside her textbooks. She smiled, thinking about the lovely gift. It was so romantic.

She picked up Zeus at Mallory's and they spoke briefly. The radio station hadn't called her, it turned out. Kim decided not to say anything to Mallory about the invitation. At least not yet. Finally, she and Zeus entered her own townhome next door.

"You're getting me into a lot of trouble," she said. Zeus looked up at her, curious.

The landlord was gone. The sink appeared to be fixed, again, and she tested the garbage disposal. Satisfied, Kim rinsed her hands as Zeus sat on the floor. He never took his eyes off her.

"I can't afford another place right now, so if you get us evicted then we're just going to have to live in a cardboard box under a bridge," she said, watching his large brown eyes follow her out the kitchen and into the living room. Then, as she moved toward the phone, she hesitated and pulled out the poetry book and removed the invitation.

"*Greico's Italian Restaurant. I will be waiting.*"

She found the Yellow Pages phone book and flipped through it. Finding the number for Greico's Italian Fine Cuisine, she dialed the number.

"*Pleasant evening. Thank you for calling Greico's Italian Fine Cuisine. What can I do for you this evening?*" came the voice over the phone.

"My name is Kimberly Bradford..." She absent mindedly looped a finger between the black spirals of the twisted phone cord. "I need to confirm reservations for, um, Ross McGuire."

"Yes, of course. For what evening Miss Bradford."

"I'm not sure. Possibly tonight."

"One moment, Miss Bradford..." Kim could hear the rattling of paper and a moment later the voice returned. *"I'm sorry ma'am. I show no reservations in that name. However..."*

"Yes?"

"Reservations have been made in your name for eight o'clock Friday evening."

An overwhelming giddy feeling rippled through Kim's body and she hung up the phone. She returned to the kitchen and sat down at the table, her dog lying at her feet.

Zeus whimpered and looked away. She smiled fondly at him then unfolded the newspaper she had started to read this morning, glancing at the bold headline describing the Congressman's murder. The ringing phone broke her concentration. Sighing, she looked at Zeus.

The phone rang again.

Huffing, Zeus leapt up to his feet and trotted out the room.

"I know! I know. It's not your fault." Returning to the living room, she reached for the receiver. "Hello?"

There was no answer. Only breathing.

"Is someone there?"

A quiet, masculine voice rippled across the line. He read the poem to her, *"If You Forget Me."* Static crackled again, then the line went silent.

"Ross…?"

He didn't answer.

"Ross," she whispered again. She picked up the poetry book. Flipping through the pages, she found the poem he just recited. "If You Forget Me," Kim continued. "That's Pablo Neruda. Twenty Love Poems and a Song of Despair."

Static crackled again.

"Did you give me that book?" she asked.

The line clicked and a dial tone blared through the receiver. He was gone.

Five weeks and fifteen hours. She wanted to scream. Kim hung up the receiver, took a deep breath, calmed herself. She picked it back up. Dialed caller return. Waited.

The phone rang.

It rang again, then a recorded voice stated, *"Sorry. That number has been blocked."*

Frustrated, she hung up the phone. *If Ross was reaching out to her*, she thought, *maybe she could run down to his job at the garage. Maybe he wanted her to.* Again, she didn't want to look desperate, and decided to wait until Friday. She could play his game.

Kim glanced around the room, considering for a moment calling Mallory, then remembered her friend's dinner engagement with Addison and *that* shrink.

6

Element of Surprise

Tuesday, January 11, 2000
10:32 AM

    With no classes till early afternoon, Kim slept late the next morning. She was finally woken when Mallory, standing on her front porch, rang the doorbell. Calming Zeus, she opened the door and let her neighbor inside.

    "You promised me lunch," Mallory said, pushing past Kim and entering the living room.

    "I don't think so," Kim closed and tied her robe. The poetry book still sat on the old recliner next to the scrapbook. The invitation to Greico's lay beside the phone.

    "Yes, you did." Mallory twirled around, facing her. Zeus whined, vying for her attention, and she pet him on top his head. She glanced at Kim. "You know, for skipping out on Addison's birthday celebration last night."

Kim shut the front door. "You mean at Greico's Italian Restaurant..."

"Of course. He turned fifty." Mallory laughed, flipping her red hair. Zeus cocked his head, watching her. "Now get dressed. Gunz is treating us."

"The baseball player?" Kim looked confused. "He's still in town?"

"For a whole week." Mallory explained as if the answer was obvious. She turned and made her way up the spiral staircase to the bedroom loft. Zeus followed her. "His team is playing in some kind of game for sick children. I think they have cancer or something."

"But what about Addison?" Kim ran upstairs after her.

"Oh, he's fine. He doesn't have any kids."

"Your date," Kim clarified. "How was your date?"

"Fine. I mean, the movie was good." Mallory opened the closet doors and ran a hand along the line of clothes. She scrutinized all the navy and tan skirts, blouses and slacks crammed into the four-by-two cubby the landlord jokingly referred to as a closet. "Maybe not as good as the one with Julia Roberts and Richard Gere... Have you seen the one where she runs out of her own wedding wearing that white gown and riding a horse?"

"Wait..." Kim started, but hesitated. She watched Mallory select a blouse and flip it off the hanger.

Shaking her head, Kim's mind raced, focused

on the Pablo Neruda poetry book and the invitation to Greico's Italian Restaurant. For a moment, she considered telling Mallory about them. Instead, she reached for the blouse in Mallory's hands, and said simply, "Okay, but I have classes this afternoon."

Forty-five minutes later, the girls parked down town, a block away from a corner diner called The Fork and Spoon. Mallory hadn't stopped talking about the baseball player since leaving the townhome community. She prattled on about his accomplishments, his RBI average, his wins, his all-star selection.

"And did I tell you he has nineteen inch arms?" Mallory placed a dime in the parking meter. "How do I know, you ask. Because I measured them."

Finally, as she led Kim down the block toward the diner, she mentioned Dr. Alec Whitman.

"Now, don't be mad..." Mallory said. She placed a hand on Kim's shoulder, as if to calm her. "I told you the doctor wanted to apologize personally for standing you up."

"You didn't." Kim hesitated before stepping through the swinging door. She realized she had just been ambushed. "And I told you, he's not a doctor."

When they passed the front counter, Mallory shrieked in surprise and dropped her purse. Kim abruptly stepped back, then turned her head toward the booth in the back. Addison Gaynor was standing there, holding up his arm and motioning to his watch.

"Addison," Kim said. She picked up Mallory's purse from the floor.

"Time is of the essence, ladies." He stepped aside allowing Kim to slip into the booth. Mallory

JC Gatlin

remained standing, looking at Addison, then back at the diner entrance, then at Addison again.

"Wha---" Mallory stammered. She could barely speak. "Wha--"

"What am I doing here?" he asked for her. "Mallory, my dear, what's gotten into you? You can barely speak."

Kim glanced at him then back at Mallory, who was turning pale.

"Are you ill?" he continued. "You don't look well."

Mallory looked at the front door then toward the street. Gunz would be here any second. She looked back at Addison. "What?"

Fed up, Kim pushed Mallory aside and extended a hand to Addison. "It's good to see you, Addison. Happy fiftieth birthday."

When the waitress arrived, Kim ordered two salads with diet sodas as Addison shifted his bifocals to the edge of his nose and studied the menu. He craned his neck and squinted his eyes before finally deciding on a fish taco, then changed his mind and splurged on a hamburger with cheese and bacon. *Cholesterol be damned.* He laughed as he set his laptop computer on the table and unfolded it open. It hummed as it booted up, and he scratched the graying beard on his chin as he waited.

Mallory watched this, then took a deep breath, as if to collect her composure again.

"So, Pudd'n Toes, tell me. Just what are you doing here? Now? Just what are you doing here now?" Mallory's eyes were glued to the windows, watching the street.

Addison's eyes lifted from his laptop. "Why I'm

having lunch, of course. And I almost didn't make it. It seems I misplaced my wallet this morning, but fortunately, some chap found it and deposited it in the building's lost and found."

"What are you doing *here* though?" Mallory asked again, urgency rising in her voice. In any second, Gunz would walk through that door and be at this table.

"Dr. Whitman said that he planned to meet you girls for lunch," he explained.

Kim shook her head, then shot Mallory one of her patented killer glares. Addison continued.

"Regrettably however he received, yet again, an urgent phone call from a troubled patient and asked that I inform you that he would be unable to accompany us." Addison grinned. *Did he know what Mallory was up to?*

The thought flashed through Kim's head, and she clarified, "Another troubled patient."

"Fortunately for us all, I encountered the good doctor," he offered. "Our agencies occupy and operate in the same building, you see."

"He could have called," Mallory said.

"He left a message on your answering machine." His eyes returned to the laptop screen as his voice lowered to a soft mutter. He seemed to be done with the conversation. "I'm sure he assumed you..."

Mallory cut him off. "Then *you* could have called."

"You don't have a mobile phone." He sounded exasperated. The food arrived, and he spread out a napkin and placed it in his lap. "So it wouldn't have done any good for me to leave you a message as well, would it?"

Mallory muttered incoherently, turning to Kim then back to Addison then back to Kim. Addison continued.

"Dr. Whitman's patient was apparently upset about the Congressman's murder." His eyes enlarged and focused on Mallory, but she clearly wasn't listening. He cleared his throat, then turned to Kim. "Have you read the papers? The whole town is in an uproar."

"I know, it was just horrible," Kim said. She took a nervous bite of salad. "Just horrible."

"It's scandalous, is what it is. Just scandalous." Addison leaned across the table, as if to speak privately to Kim. "He was murdered, just like his brother twenty-five years ago."

"What?" Kim put down her fork.

"The Congressman's brother was murdered twenty-five years ago," Addison explained. "He was a senior in high school and on a date with a freshman girl. She disappeared, but the boy was found dead."

"Oh, Pudd'n Toes, that's an urban legend." Mallory sat back. "Like the Hook Man or the Skunk Ape."

"I thought that high school boy was attacked by a gator." Kim's voice held a rasp of excitement. Shifting in the booth, she folded her arms across her chest and turned her head, returning her gaze out the window. Her mouth fell open when she saw him, Antonio 'The Gunz' Gonzales, standing on the other side of the street, waiting to cross. She kicked Mallory's shin under the table, getting her attention.

Pointing out the window, she mouthed "The Gunz." Mallory crinkled her nose, staring puzzled at her. Then her red head turned to the window and she choked on her salad.

"Pudd'n Toes," she said, looking up at Addison. "Let's go somewhere else to eat."

Addison forced an uncomfortably chuckle from his throat that signaled he neither appreciated nor agreed with her suggestion. "Mal, dear, the food just arrived. What's the matter with you?"

"We should really go somewhere healthier to eat." Urgency rose in Mallory's voice. "The food here is really greasy and considering your age now and your high cholesterol..."

He ignored her. Kim interrupted.

"How are the murders connected? Do they know who did it?" she asked him, purposely delaying any chance for a clean getaway. Kim watched Mallory squirm, then noticed the traffic light had changed outside the window. Gunz was crossing the street.

"Addison," Mallory said quickly. Smoke was practically coming out of her ears as her brain scrambled to find a solution. "Is that your car alarm?"

Addison paused, concentrating. "I don't hear anything. Surely you must be mistaken. I parked over a block away."

"Your car alarm is very distinctive. I'm positive I hear it. What do you think, Kim?" Mallory continued.

Kim was focused on the window. Gunz had crossed the street and was approaching the diner. Mallory slammed her drink on the table, splashing diet soda and getting Kim's attention. "Kimberly Bradford, do you hear Addison's car alarm?"

Kim wiped diet soda from her sleeve. "The alarm?" she said quietly at first, then suddenly understood. "Yes! Yes, I think I do hear your car alarm. It's very distinctive!"

Addison leapt up from the table.

"Not my BMW." His voice echoed through the diner and the people in the booths across from them stopped talking and looked up.

Mallory leaned forward. "Go check on it, right now before some teenage hoodlums run off with your hubcaps!"

Addison nodded at her then sprinted toward the entrance, leaving his laptop on the table. As he made his way out, he passed Gunz Gonzales and ran into the street. Cars honked as he ran down the block.

A moment later, Gunz entered the diner and found Kim and Mallory sitting at a booth.

"Chica," he said, taking Mallory's hand and kissing it. "Pleasure to see me again."

"Yes," Mallory said, pulling her hand away. "It's always a pleasure to see me too."

"Sorry so late." He leaned toward her for a kiss. "Press for the charity exhibition game went long this morning."

Mallory pointed a finger at him. "Well you're a naughty, naughty boy, mister. And I'm afraid you've missed lunch. Kim and I were just leaving."

Mallory grabbed her purse and shifted out the booth. She looked at Kim, waiting for her to follow. Gunz looked at Kim, then down at her untouched salad. Kim smiled apologetically, then scooted out the booth and stood next to Mallory.

"When we see again?" he asked as Mallory threw a five-dollar bill down on the table and bolted toward the door.

"Swing by my place tonight," she said, turning back to him and grinning devilishly. "Naughty, naughty boy. You're gonna get a spanky!"

Gunz grinned and his ears turned red. He placed his hands in his pockets, then looked back at the table. The fiver had landed on the laptop. He started to call after the girls, but they were gone. A waitress moved to the table, picking up the five-dollar bill and stuffed it into the money pouch around her waist. Then she noticed the computer.

"That yours?" she asked.

Gunz shook his head and stepped away, moving toward the men's room.

As the waitress picked up the plates of uneaten salad and nearly full glasses of diet soda, Addison scrambled back into the diner. He ran to the table and grabbed his laptop.

"What are you doing?" he said to the waitress with an accusatory tone. The woman paused, holding the dishes, and glared at him.

"I'm campaigning for re-election. What do you think I'm doing?"

Addison ignored the sarcasm. "What happened to the ladies who were accompanying this booth?"

"Ladies? That's a laugh." The waitress chuckled and turned her back, walking into the kitchen.

Closing his laptop, Addison looked around the coffee shop. The girls were gone. Perplexed, he rubbed his bearded chin.

His pocket vibrated, startling him, and he removed a cellular phone from his jacket. Flipping it open, he brought it to his left ear. It was Dr. Whitman on the other end.

"You just missed the girls," Addison said, then paused as he listened.

"Unfortunately I'm at a loss," he continued. "They just abruptly departed. But I informed Kimberly of your regrets and that you were detained once again by an unstable patient."

He glanced toward the front entry. The lug of a baseball player who had been pursuing Mallory was exiting the diner. Addison paused a moment, watching him, then turned his attention back to the phone.

"No, Alec. I don't know if Mallory has said anything to Kimberly yet... but I'm most certain she will."

7
A Close Call

"That was close." Mallory laughed, pushing Kim out the diner doors and onto the sidewalk. They crossed the intersection against the light and headed back to Mallory's parked Miata. Making it clear that she was not pleased, Kim walked several steps ahead. She crossed her arms, swinging her purse. Mallory caught up to her, telling her to slow down.

Kim picked up her pace. "I can't believe you tried to set me up with that old psychologist again. You just don't know when to quit, do you?"

"He's a psychiatrist, and…" Mallory grabbed her arm to slow her down. "Stop being so melodramatic."

"Melodramatic?" Kim whipped around to confront her friend face to face. "Not only did you ambush me, but this is the second time he's stood me up - second time in a row!"

"He just got detained with another crazy patient, that's all." Mallory punctuated that with a light, throaty chuckle. "The whole town is freaked out over the Congressman's murder so it's understandable."

"You're changing the subject." Kim turned and stepped off the sidewalk into the street. She headed toward the car parallel parked in front of a meter. Mallory followed her into the oncoming traffic.

"Would you just wait?" She grabbed Kim's arm again. Mallory stopped her in the middle of the street. A car honked and swerved around them. Oblivious, Kim pointed a finger at her and leaned forward.

"You sandbagged me with another blind date. You know I'm involved."

"Ross went M.I.A. on you, what, six weeks ago? He's gone." Another car blared its horn. Mallory waved it away. "I just wanted to get your mind off it. Besides, Dr. Whitman has lined up a very exciting date."

"You just don't give up, do you?"

"Listen to me, Kim. He's really been putting a lot of pressure on me lately. He's talked about you for ages and he's been asking me to set you two up for a long time. Ever since..."

Breaks squeaked on a truck as it swerved to miss them. Kim ignored it. "Ever since what, Mallory? Since Ross dumped me?"

"No - since Ross disappeared." Mallory paused. Her eyes softened and a faint smile crossed her lips. "Kim, he's not coming back."

Kim was about to protest. It was a knee-jerk reaction to tell Mallory how wrong she was. For a moment, Kim considered explaining about the mysterious poems and the invitation for dinner on Friday night. She wanted to tell Mallory about the phone calls. All those cryptic messages and notes – it had to be from Ross. It just had to be. They were meant for each other.

Instead Kim looked down at her feet and sighed. "I'm just not in the mood to be sweet and sociable. You know what I mean? I'm angry. And I want to hit something. I want to rip something apart and stomp on it and crush it and..."

Another car honked and the driver screamed obscenities as he whizzed past. The girls were unfazed standing in the center of the road.

"Exactly my point." Mallory snapped her fingers, seemingly very pleased with herself. "That's why this handsome, debonair doctor suggested a double date at a mock war camp."

"A what?"

"A mock war camp," Mallory repeated. "Instead of miniature golf or going to a movie, we'd play weekend warrior."

Kim hesitated, watching her a moment, then followed. "What kind of date is that?"

"The kind that'll get you over Ross!" Mallory headed toward her Miata parked at the curb.

Unlocking the car door, she paused and leaned against the hood. She turned back toward Kim. "It's the kind of date where you can be tank girl and rip men apart and blow them away and stomp on them... only with paint pellets." Mallory's eyes enlarged and she took a breath, as if waiting for Kim to protest. When she didn't, Mallory continued. "He's a head shrink, Kim. He knows about these kind of things."

Kim opened the passenger side door. "I just don't think..."

"Listen to me. What better way to release all this pent up emotion than by shooting macho guys in camouflage with red paint balls?" Mallory insisted. "It's what you need right now. I think it would really do you a lot of good."

Kim watched Mallory a moment, then slipped into the car. "Is this a date?"

"It's anything you want it to be."

Kim hesitated, biting her lower lip, then continued walking again. "No," she said. "Ross is coming back to me. He left me a..."

"Too little, too late. Besides, I've already signed you up." Mallory fastened her seatbelt and put the key into the ignition. "So really, the only question left is --- Who should I ask to go on this weekend excursion? The wealthy and distinguished Addison Gaynor or the tall, dark and exciting ball player Gunz Gonzales?"

Kim hesitated again. "Mallory, since we're being completely honest with each other, I've got some thing to tell you..."

"Decisions. Decisions." Mallory continued as Kim wasn't even there. She backed out of the parking spot. "Sometimes I wish I was more like you. Then I wouldn't ever have to worry about men."

Driving west toward the university campus, Mallory rambled on like she always did, and Kim considered telling her that if Addison and this Alec Whitman were such good friends, it made little sense to take her secret ball playing lover. But like any good friend, Kim let Mallory have her fantasy. And, so that she could keep her own, Kim decided to let the upcoming dinner date remain a secret. A secret only shared with Ross.

Their secret rendezvous.

It was all she thought about that afternoon in class. The Professor had moved on from Cyrano de Bergerac. The odd boy dressed in black still glared at her though, tossing daggers with his eyes. She didn't care. Her mind was elsewhere.

* * * * * * *

Ross' invitation to dinner still weighed heavy on her mind when she entered the old folks home and Nurse Carla, wearing her aqua-colored scrubs, holding a clipboard in one hand and waving with the other, called out. "Miss Bradford, your grandaddy isn't feeling so well today. He hasn't gotten out of bed yet."

Kim paused. "Is he okay?"

"You know how it is, child. He's got his good days and bad days," she said. "He didn't touch his peas and carrots last night, but he still had a solid bowel movement."

"Glad to hear it." Kim waved a hand, moving down the hallway. "I'm going to go check on him."

"That's good, child!" Carla called after her. "That's good for him. He likes visitors."

The door was shut when Kim made it to his

room, and she creaked it open to peek inside. His room was stuffy and warm, unusually dark with the curtains drawn.

"Grampa?" she asked, allowing her eyes to adjust.

He was lying in bed, chin up, staring at the ceiling. She slipped into the room and shut the door behind her. Approaching the bed, she reached for him and took his hand.

"Grampa, the nurse said you're not feeling well today." Kim watched him a moment, then put a hand on his forehead. "You're not running a fever. Why didn't you eat your peas and carrots?"

Without turning his head, his eyes moved toward her. She smiled at him. But there was no recognition. He looked back up at the ceiling.

Thinking he might be too warm, she folded down the heavy quilt, freeing his arms but keeping his legs and feet covered. Her grandmother had made that quilt, and it looked similar to the one draped over the recliner back home. Then Kim stepped to the window and opened the curtains. She could feel the draft coming through the window panes along with the warmth of the sun. Grampa flinched slightly in bed as sunlight filled the room.

"Now isn't that better?" Kim asked, turning to him. She then walked over to the television sitting on top the dresser and turned it on. She flipped through the channels twisting the knob beside the screen.

"Let's liven it up a bit in here," she said.

She turned the stations, but found nothing worth watching. Propped up against the side of the television, three black, rectangular VHS cassette tapes collected dust. With blue magic marker, one was labeled "*MR. ED, THE TALKING HORSE*," the other two were marked "*I LOVE LUCY*." She picked up one labeled "LUCY" and pushed it into the VCR. She then turned the station to channel three.

Glancing back to her grandfather, she smiled at him again. "You want to watch Lucy?"

From the bed, he watched her but didn't answer. His eyes were fixed on the TV. The screen went black before the familiar gray heart appeared and the theme song crackled through the speakers. Kim moved over to the bed and sat down beside him on the edge. Leaning toward him, she wrapped her arms around his frail shoulder and put her cheek next to his. "Life doesn't get any easier," she whispered. "We just get stronger."

She squeezed him as they watched the show. Lucy mistakenly thinks Ethel is the female bank robber she just heard about on the news, and hatches a plot to catch her in the act. Watching, Kim laughed.

For the first time in a while, she felt warm inside. She felt like the little girl who would climb in her Grampa's lap when he was trying to read the newspaper, and he would turn on old reruns to appease her and she would curl up beside him, and they would laugh together.

Glancing at her grandfather, now a thin, wisp of an aged, fragile shell lying in bed, she noticed something else. Something she hadn't seen in a long time. Her grandfather was laughing too.

A little over an hour and three episodes later, Kim left the nursing home. She had to stop at the grocery store and was away longer than expected. Still, despite the time and the heavy bag of groceries in her arms, Kim took the long way home.

She walked along Morris Munger Road.

Coming to the sharp bend, she set her bag of groceries down on the shoulder. Noticing an ant hill, she decided to move the grocery bag, then ran along the side of the road to the weathered real estate sign. She searched around it, and then a few feet further away.

Cars whizzed past her on the street, and Kim laughed at herself. She had walked along this shoulder so many times over the last few weeks, searching this area time and time again, that she imagined getting struck by a hit and run and dying right here on the road. She would probably become a tormented ghost, she thought, roaming this haunted highway, searching for an eternity. Never finding it, but always looking. Kim shuddered at the thought as darkness encroached. It was time to give up for the day, and go home.

When she finally made it back to the gated community and approached her townhome, she saw Zeus' arrow-shaped head staring at her through the front bay window. His ears pointed, his paws on the glass, he was waiting like a sentinel and barked as she approached the front door. Yelling at him to pipe down and fishing for her keys, she removed a flyer rubber-banned to the doorknob. It was from a cheap Chinese dive around the corner. Tossing it into the bag on top a loaf of bread, she unlocked the door and Zeus greeted her as if she had been gone a year.

Or at least five weeks, one day and fifteen hours.

* * * * * * *

Next door, inside Mallory's dark townhome, a man stood at the upstairs window, watching. He had been waiting for Kimberly to walk through the gated entry. When she did, he studied her approach. She walked slowly past the front gates and parking lot with school books and a bag of groceries in her arms.

He wondered if the poetry book he'd given her was among them.

Balancing the books and groceries in one arm, her other arm disappeared into the purse strapped around her right shoulder. He knew she was fumbling for her keys. There was a matching set hanging on the keyhook downstairs by Mallory's front door.

The thought made him smile as he watched Kim finally pull her key chain from the purse and then reposition the grocery bag and school books. With so much fuss, she headed to the porch and approached her front door. She yelled something to her dog, something he couldn't hear from his perch above. But he could imagine what she was saying.

He shut his eyes. "If you forget me," he said. "There is something I want you to know."

* * * * * * *

Zeus whimpered as Kim set down her school books and took the bag of groceries into the kitchen.

He came trotting after her, holding his thin leather leash in his mouth.

"I know. I know." She took the leash and wrapped the collar around his neck. "I've been gone all day."

The words were barely out of her mouth when Zeus' ears perked up. He instantly turned his head toward the front door. There was a soft bump. Then the jiggle of the knob. Zeus barked and ran to the door.

Kim followed, as the door knob turned. It sounded like someone was trying to unlock the door.

Zeus barked and jumped at the door as Kim put her face up to the peep hole. There was a man standing there on the porch. Startled, she stepped back and the Doberman growled. Kim opened the door.

"Whoa," he said holding out his hand. It was Addison Gaynor. "Please accept my apology if I startled you, Kimberly. And, please, forgive my unannounced intrusion."

"What were you doing here?"

"Looking for Mallory," he said quickly, seeming to brush-off her question. He nervously raised a hand and swept his fingers through his graying hair. A key ring looped around his index finger jingled and a house key tapped his cheek.

Kim noticed this immediately. Embarrassed, he lowered his hand, hiding the silver ring of keys in his palm. Kim stared at his fist and pressed him for an answer.

"Were you inside her house?"

"She isn't home." He shook his head and stepped forward. Kim blocked the door with her body, holding him at the threshold. She asked again.

"Were you in her house?"

"She gave me keys, but no. I've been waiting for her in my BMW," he said, then added, "She's seeing another man, isn't she?"

"I don't know," Kim said. Zeus whimpered, reminding her that he was in pain. He had to go, *now.* She clutched the leash and held the dog between them. "Maybe she's working late."

"She works at home." Addison persisted.

Kim looked down at Zeus, who was staring longingly at a newly planted tree. "I don't know where she is or what she's doing. Listen, I don't mean to be rude, but..."

Addison cut her off. "I've waited for her all afternoon, ever since you two disappeared on me at the diner. Let me just wait in your home until she returns."

"No, I don't think that's a good idea." Holding tight to the leash, Kim kept Zeus from running. Across the street on the sidewalk, Mrs. Roundtree was walking Little Rosie. Zeus noticed this too, as his body suddenly stiffened and pointed toward the offending Pekingese.

Addison glanced behind him in their direction, then turned back to Kimberly. "I've got to know who she's with."

"No, Addison..." Kim started. Zeus growled at the Pekingese, then turned toward the tree and whimpered. He looked up at Kim, then suddenly noticed Little Rosie again and growled. Kim tightened her grip on the leash and shook her head at Addison. "What are you doing? Are you spying on her?"

"I know, I'm becoming obsessive again," he said, finally taking a step back. "I'll depart."

He turned and stepped away from them.

Kim watched him return to the curb and slip inside his red BMW. The headlights came on and the car quietly pulled away.

When he was finally out of sight, she let go of the leash. Like a rocket, Zeus scrambled into the parking lot, barking at Mrs. Roundtree and Little Rosie. Then he stopped abruptly, almost stumbling over his feet, and changed course to his favorite tree.

8

Invitations from the Dead & Gone

Wednesday, January 12, 2000
11:12 AM

"You were out with the baseball player last night." Kim studied Mallory sitting on the edge of the bed in her loft, and shot her a disapproving smile. "Weren't you?"

"Of course." Mallory nodded and ran a hand over the ripples in the bedspread. She had dropped by to talk Kim into lunch again. But Kim requested a favor instead. Now, Mallory turned her head and crinkled her nose. "Why?"

"Because Addison almost caught you, and I had to cover. That's why." Kim stood at her small closet trying on a red dress that showed off her legs. Ross had always said that it was his favorite. She hadn't worn it since he left, but today was different. She finally decided to head into downtown Stillwater to confront him at the garage. She had no choice, really. No one knew where he was staying since he moved out five weeks ago. *Five weeks, two days and seven hours*. But above all else, she just wanted to get past all the childish notes and poems. And what was the deal with the invitation to dinner on Friday night? But, she couldn't think about that right now. For the moment, she focused on Mallory's problems. "I think Addison is stalking you."

"So? Let him." Mallory motioned for Kim to turn around and pose. Studying her, Mallory shook her head in disgust and leapt off the bed toward the closet. Flipping through dresses on hangers, she continued, "I don't care what Addison thinks."

"Well, you were pretty worried about him catching you at lunch yesterday." Kim slipped out of the red dress and folded it on the edge of the bed.

Deciding on a sheer white chiffon cocktail dress with sequined straps, Mallory squealed, pulled it out of the closet and handed it to Kim.

Kim folded her arms and shook her head. It looked more like a slip, than a dress. "That's one of *your* dresses."

"It's Chanel and it's very expensive," Mallory said, dejected, and returned it to the closet. "I knew I liked it for a reason."

"I'm not wearing that."

Mallory hesitated, as if really analyzing the assortment of blouses, slacks and sweaters hanging in Kim's small closet, then turned to face her.

"Gunz is fun and he enjoys the simple pleasures of life," Mallory said. Her eyes sparkled as she talked. "When Addison left the other night, Gunz came over and took me for a walk and we looked at the lights along Black Moon Lake. Isn't that just the most romantic thing you've ever heard?"

Mallory noticed the red dress folded on the edge of the bed and walked past Kim to pick it up. Holding it in her hands, she studied it a moment then handed it to Kim.

"Now this is hot," she offered. "When you walk in wearing this, every grease monkey in that garage is going to flip out from under the car he's working on and whistle."

Kim rolled her eyes, taking the dress. She slipped back into it just as Zeus' ears perked up. He raised his head, then leapt to his feet and scrambled down the spiral staircase barking. Kim looked after him as Mallory sighed. "Now what?"

A loud knock interrupted them, and Kim came downstairs to find Zeus barking and jumping at the front door. Mallory followed.

"I'm being serious," she continued, seemingly oblivious to the commotion at the front door. "Ross is going to be putty in your hands."

Holding her dog back with one hand, Kim unlocked and opened the door with the other. The landlord was standing on the porch. Wearing his dirty blue jeans overalls, he held his straw hat in one hand and, with the other, ran a handkerchief over his bald head to wipe away the sweat.

"Missy," he said. "Hope I'm not bothering you."

Kim held Zeus by the collar. Barking and growling, he snapped at the man's hand. Kim yanked him back.

"We were just about to leave," she said.

"Well, I won't keep you." He put the

handkerchief in the center pocket of his overalls. "I was fixing the plumbing across the street at Mrs. Roundtree's residence and just wanted to let you know I'd be turning the water off for about an hour."

Zeus was howling now, leaping up on his hind paws. Kim swatted him on the nose, then turned back to the landlord.

"No worries," she said. "We'll be gone for a while."

"Good to hear." He looked down at the growling Doberman. Zeus snapped at him again. Shaking his head, he looked back at Kim. "One of these days I'm adding a no pets clause to your lease."

Kim told him goodbye and shut the door. Zeus instantly calmed and Kim towered over him, putting her hands to her hips.

"Bad dog," she scolded. "If you get us kicked out of here, you're going to live in a kennel. Do you want to live in a kennel?"

Zeus whimpered at her as Mallory handed her a pair of shoes. "Let's go kick Ross' ass," she said.

Within the hour, they were headed out in Mallory's little Miata. Rolling along Morris Munger Road, Kim stared out the passenger-side window, noticing they were coming up to the bend. Mallory swerved into the curve, and Kim stared at the old real estate sign, then glanced at the empty wooden fruit stand.

She was focused on the window, staring intently, and Mallory seemed to notice this.

"Did I tell you that Gunz is in love with me?" Mallory asked as she shifted gears. "He may even ask me to marry him, he's so in love with me."

"You just met him!" Kim was sitting in the seat beside her. Her mind had been on Ross, and what she would say to him. She'd been so focused, she hadn't noticed that neither had said a word since pulling out of the townhome parking lot. However, Mallory's sudden statement caught her off guard.

"It's perfect," Mallory explained. "I could travel with the baseball team. I'd be, like, a groupie or something. Doesn't that sound exciting?"

"Mallory Astin, are you crazy? You hate sports and you hate traveling… And, hello, you just met the man."

"Details," Mallory answered, her red hair whipping in the wind. She turned onto Main Street and passed the University campus. "Minor Details."

"What about Addison? I get the impression from him that you two are in a serious, monogamous relationship."

"Addison gets on my nerves." Mallory laughed again and then mocked him using a nasal voice. "We're always in a *fantastic hurry* or everything is just *simply scandalous*."

Kim shrugged her shoulders, looking out the passenger window again. Giant magnolia trees lined the median that ran along Main Street, and on either side stood store fronts that were built in the late nineteen-thirties. She turned back to Mallory. "So, you're breaking up with Addison?"

"Hell, no! Have you seen his home? I'd kill to live in that place."

"But what about the baseball player?"

"He's going to be on the road all the time. I can't live like that."

"You're incorrigible. This is exactly why Addison

is stalking you," Kim said. "I don't want to hear anymore about Gunz Gonzales and his sixteen inch, er, guns."

"They're nineteen inch, but whatever." Mallory corrected her as she turned off Main and came to a four way stop. "Look, so we're almost there. You're walking into the garage looking like all that and a bag chips, all the mechanics are drooling, Ross can't believe his eyes... then what?"

"What do you mean?"

"I mean, what are you going to say to the slug when you see him?"

"I don't know. I hadn't thought that far ahead." She was lying though. It's actually all she had thought about for the last five weeks. She chewed her bottom lip, considering the question.

She'd doubted herself since the night he left. That night five weeks ago when Ross pulled his Camero to the side of the road and she stormed out, slamming the car door. It would be the last time she'd see him.

The last time she'd *ever* see him.

* * * * * * *

They were both in high school when they first met. He was a senior; she a sophomore. They had separate classes and separate friends, until one fateful night when they were both in separate cars headed west across the Courtney Campbell

Causeway over Tampa Bay.

It was Saturday evening, and Ross was riding shotgun in a silver gray Lincoln Town Car. It belonged to his best friend's mother, but they had it for the night. The stereo was cranked up, windows down. When a red convertible --- top down, two hot girls in the front seat, three in the back --- pulled up alongside them on the bridge, Ross' buddy honked.

Ross leaned over his buddy to yell to the girls from the driver's side window. They honked back and laughed. One blew kisses, and Ross' buddy grinned and lewdly flashed his tongue. Ross followed that with yelling again out the driver's side window. "Where you headed?"

The girls couldn't hear him over the rush of the wind as they sped along the bridge. He yelled again. But it was no use.

His buddy pushed him off him and nudged him back to his side of the car. He almost lost control of the steering wheel, and the town car drifted into the girl's path. They blared the horn and girls erupted into squeals and giggles. Ross leaned over his buddy again and yelled for them to follow. That's when his eyes made contact with the dark haired girl in the back seat.

Her eyes locked with his, and she smiled back at him.

Ross yelled something to her, just as his buddy threw his left arm out the window motioning to the car-load of girls to follow. With both their heads turned, eyes firmly planted on the red convertible, they were oblivious to the traffic ahead. It had stopped on the bridge, and the Lincoln Town Car slammed into the back bumper of the car in front of them.

Metal bolted with a loud thud and the impact threw both Ross and his buddy forward into the steering wheel. It was a minor accident, but the rear-ended driver leapt out of his car with his pants ablaze, ready to tie into the boys.

The girls in the convertible laughed and continued down the bridge. Except for Kim.

She demanded that they pull over. She was worried about the cute guys in the other car and wanted to make sure they were alright. So they pulled over to the narrow shoulder on the bridge, and Kim got out of the car.

Walking back to the accident, she found Ross and his buddy. Steam was boiling out of the radiator, as well as the ears of the driver with the dented back bumper. Kim approached them and Ross introduced himself.

He smiled at her, and she smiled back.

They were speaking casually in the school hallways between classes at first; she would wait for him after shop class and he would walk her home. By the semester's end, he gave her his class ring. She looped a gold chain through it and wore it proudly around her neck to signify that they were now dating, officially.

Kim brought Ross home to meet her parents, and her father took an immediate dislike to him. "He's going to break your heart," Kim's father predicted. "He's a grease monkey and there's no future with a grease monkey."

Kim laughed and ignored her father's warning. "We're just dating," she said. "I'm not marrying the guy."

But her father's prediction came true, and Ross broke her heart – *for the first time* -- during their prom night. She had planned to give him her virginity in a beautiful hotel suite with rose petals on the bed; he wanted to go bar hopping with his buddies. She vowed never to speak to him again, ripped the necklace from her throat and flung his class ring at him. They were now over, officially.

Kim cried to her friends and to her parents. But when she didn't receive the support she was looking for, she called her Grampa. He listened to her carry-on over the phone for a solid hour, then calmly told her, "Life won't get any easier, darling. But you'll get a hell of a lot stronger."

A few weeks passed and Ross reconciled with Kim just in time for graduation. This time, he didn't give her the class ring. Instead, he gave her a Doberman pincer puppy and told her he loved her and wanted to spend the rest of their lives together. He wrote her a beautiful love letter, a poem really. And, it took Kim's breath away. She named the puppy Zeus and took both boys into her arms.

"I can't believe you could write such beautiful poetry," she gushed. "It's so unlike you."

"You make me a better man," he said, kissing her. It was all the explanation she needed.

Their first summer after high school, that first summer as adults, was the best time of her life. They had fun. They made love. And they made plans for the future. But the end of summer brought devastating news: a routine X-ray showed a suspicious shadow on her mother's left breast.

It was nothing, Kim was told. The doctors were

being overly cautious. And the way her mother worked out, took care of herself and ate properly, it had to be nothing. It certainly couldn't be cancer…

But it *was* cancer. And her mother grew seriously ill.

Kimberly and her father focused on her mother's health and comfort. It consumed Kim's attention and Ross couldn't handle it. He moved on to another girl with more time on her hands and less drama in her life. Kim didn't care. She didn't have time to care. She wasn't going to let cancer take her mother…

But it did, in the space of a few months.

Nor did it stop there. As the disease ate her mother from the inside out, it also ate away at her father's soul. He was no longer the headstrong family man who built furniture and bird houses in the garage, loved the Florida Gators, pre-dawn fishing trips and his wife and daughter.

When the agent for the insurance company came knocking on their door, her father refused to speak with him. He didn't want to talk about final benefits and told the man to get out of his house.

The agent was understandably surprised, and he left the check on the kitchen table. It sat there long after the man left, and for days until Kim couldn't stand it any longer.

She pleaded with her father to get help and dragged him to grief counseling. Together, they talked to a patient, understanding psychiatrist named Natalie, who was a widow herself. She had the brightest blue eyes Kim had ever seen.

"Your mother's in a better place," Natalie told them. But it offered little comfort to her father.

His heart withered when mother died, leaving an angry, brooding shadow of the man that was. Like his mood, he now sought the dark. All the blinds remained shut, the doors locked and their home became a silent and dusty memorial. Her father found every photograph of her mother that was ever taken, and he taped them to the walls. He stayed up all night watching their wedding and vacation videos. And when he finally lost his job, the fridge sat empty until the electric company eventually turned off the power.

Still, the insurance check sat on the kitchen table, untouched.

Kim met with the grief counselor again, alone, and confided in Natalie all the details of her father's downward spiral.

"You need time to mourn and heal," Natalie told her. "You can't do that and take care of your father at the same time."

"What are you suggesting?" Kim leaned forward in the plush chair across from the psychiatrist.

"Get away for a few days." Natalie's bright eyes enlarged like saucers. "Do you have family you could visit for a while? You know, to relieve the stress?"

Kim nodded, thinking of her Grampa.

After ensuring the cupboards were stocked with cans of tuna and tomato soup, and her father was as comfortable as possible, Kim left their dark home to stay with her grandfather. He was heartbroken as well, and mourning the loss of his daughter. Kim knew that. But she also knew that he wasn't about to let her see it.

Sitting her down, he smiled at her and offered,

"Life won't get any easier, darling. But you'll get a hell of a lot stronger."

When Kim returned home a few weeks later, she found that the power had been restored, the refrigerator was full again and the bathrooms clean. The darkness had lifted. Not just within the house, but within her father too.

Even the insurance check that had been collecting dust on the kitchen table for the last few weeks had finally disappeared.

Kim was elated and thankful for the change. Her father was a new man. And to celebrate, he took her to dinner.

With Natalie.

"The shrink?" Kim couldn't believe it.

"She's a widow," he answered. "And she's surprisingly good for me."

Natalie made dinners and would set the table in the formal dining room. She used Mother's good china. She reorganized the kitchen and redecorated the family room. All her mother's knickknacks gradually disappeared, one by one. Mother could never convince her Dad to join the health club, but somehow, Natalie did. And then grocery shopping together. Then salsa dancing. A friend spotted them together late one night at the Danceteria and told Kim all about it. Every little disgusting detail.

And it didn't end there.

Kim came home one afternoon to find their framed family portrait that hung proudly over the fireplace mantle was replaced with a water color painting.

"That portrait is over ten years old," Natalie shot back. "You all have Eighties hair."

Kim didn't care. The water color painting came down and the framed family portrait went back up. But it was a futile attempt to hold onto the past, and Kim knew that. And, she knew there was no stopping the inevitable.

"We're getting married," her father told her, in the formal dining room, over a dinner served by Natalie on her mother's good china. "Your mother would want me to be happy."

Happy? Yes. Replacing *her* with their trusted shrink? Moving into *her* home and into *her* bed with *her* husband before her corpse was even cold and buried? No.

Kim was inconsolable. Until that day, she had wondered how she would ever go away to college and leave her home and her father. Now she counted down the days till she would pack-up and leave.

Once she did, she didn't look back.

The day after the wedding, Kim moved into the cozy townhome with her Grampa. He needed help with chores around the house, and needed someone to take care of him ever since Nanna passed. He paid for her to take some classes at Stillwater University.

Life was good here. She made friends with a crazy redhead named Mallory, who lived in the townhome next door. And Zeus loved to terrorize the little Pekingese that lived in the townhome across the parking lot. She also enjoyed the University; she could walk there from the townhome. In fact, she could walk almost anywhere in town – to the grocery store, to the bookstore, to the downtown restaurants. That was one of the things that she loved most about charming Stillwater. She was happy here. And even though she missed her mother and thought about her often, she felt like she was putting her life back together and moving on. Still she was lonely, and she missed Ross.

That's why, one fall afternoon while she studied in the library, Kim was so surprised to find another poem slipped inside her school books. Again, it was beautifully written.

> *"Oh, Love rips the heart in pieces,*
> > *When distance fills the empty creases*
> > *Of time*
> *And days become long stretches*
> > *Of pain and wretches*
> > *Of torment*
> > > *When our love ceases."*

Kim promptly stood up in the quiet library with a noisy, boisterous rumble and ran to the large windows. Gazing outside, she looked down on the campus to find Ross standing there on the grass. He was waiting for her with flowers in hand.

She rushed out the library, bolting down the stone steps to the lower level and rushed to the doors. Then collecting herself, she calmly stepped outside and approached him. She suppressed a smile to coldly acknowledge him.

"I made a terrible mistake," he pleaded. "Can you ever forgive me?"

Of course, she said silently in her head. Out loud, she wanted to make him suffer a little. "We shouldn't even be talking," she told him, hitting him on the shoulder. "After what you did, I can never forgive you."

But she did, and that led to passionate make-up sex in the dark, empty auditorium. The four o'clock Dramatic Arts Class interrupted them, but they snuck out undetected.

Ross moved to the small college town to be with her. She introduced him to her grandfather and to Mallory. Zeus was happy to see him again. He found a job downtown at Eddy's garage and even enrolled in a couple of classes at the University.

Kim and Ross dated again, like they were recapturing that magical summer. Everything was going great, until one fateful night when they couldn't agree on a restaurant. He wanted pizza. She wanted Italian. They both wanted to end the relationship for good.

Kim raged home, furious, vowing to never speak to him again. But when she reached the dark townhome, she knew immediately something was wrong. Zeus was upset and barking. And Grampa was lying on the linoleum floor in the kitchen, unconscious.

It was bad. Really bad. She asked the landlord to help and they rushed him to the hospital. Doctors said that her grandfather had suffered a stroke. He would need round the clock care, and would have to live in a nursing home. Kim was distraught over the news.

She watched over him at the hospital. Both the doctors and nurses urged her to go home and to get some rest, but she refused to leave her grandfather's side.

"I want to be there if he wakes up," she insisted. "We're all the family we have left."

And she watched diligently over him until he

was safely moved out of ICU into his own room and was awake again. But even then, she still spent hours and hours at the hospital. One night, she dozed off in the chair beside his hospital bed. When she woke, she found a note in her lap.

"You are the strongest, most loving woman I have ever met. You inspire me," was all it said. She knew immediately who wrote it, and who had slipped it into the room while she slept.

When she made it back home, alone, she had never been more thankful to see Ross there, waiting for her.

"I heard about what happened," he said. He kissed her, consoled her, and told her everything would be okay. The next day, he moved into the townhome with her.

Still, Ross was constantly up and down about their relationship. He left her, saying that the only way to keep her was to leave her - because he felt he needed to work on his temper, or he'd push her too far and lose her forever. That same night he changed his mind and asked her to take him back.

She did.

And they moved forward, together. Kim visited her grandfather every day in the old folks home and kept her grades up at the University. Ross worked at the garage downtown, and together they made a life for themselves, the kind Kim had always dreamed of – minus the fabulous career and penthouse apartment. Until one day, they were driving to the Dollar Store downtown.

"You know, there's actually not a lot of stuff really priced at a dollar there," Kim mentioned.

"Not possible," he said. "Everything's a dollar.

That's why they're called dollar stores."

"Not true," Kim insisted. "It's all a marketing ploy to get more people into the store."

"Then they couldn't legally call it a Dollar Store" he shot back, still trying to convince her. The fight escalated and Kim didn't speak to him for three weeks.

Once again, he left her a note professing his love and asking her to meet him at Greico's Italian Restaurant for dinner. There, he told her that she was "*The One*" and he couldn't let her walk away.

"I just don't believe the sudden change in heart," she said to him across the table, her eyes flickering in the candle light.

"It's not a change of heart," he said to her. "I've always felt this way, but I was scared."

"Scared of what?"

"Change," he said a little too quickly, then scrambled to explain himself. "Scared of growing up. Of the next step. Of the responsibility."

Kim's eyes watered, fearing that once again they had reached the impassable crossroads. "Growing up and taking on the responsibility is inevitable," she said. "It's going to happen to us whether we're prepared for it or not. Whether we want to accept it or not.

She told him she didn't want to get hurt, and he assured her he didn't want to hurt her and that she was the love of his life. That's when he got down on one knee and removed a ring from his shirt pocket.

Kim screamed, surprised and delighted, as he slipped it on her finger. It was an elegant Solitaire diamond ring with a thin, two-toned band, and it was the most beautiful thing she had ever seen. She accepted and then everyone in the restaurant applauded.

She couldn't wait to show Mallory.

Mallory of course invited them to a fancy dinner to celebrate. Addison made reservations at the most-exclusive country club in the county. Mallory was beside herself.

That night, they saw Congress William Dietz dining at a table across from them. And according to the gossip rattling through the clubhouse, Jack Nicholson and Warren Beatty were dining in the back room. Mallory asked the waiter if he had seen them.

Over a three-hundred dollar bottle of wine, they ordered dinner. Addison requested a medium-rare steak, Mallory lobster tail and Kim the veal. Ross asked them to bring him a cheeseburger and told the waiter he didn't like the wine. Please bring him a Belgian Shock Top.

Kim was furious, and told him as much. "You were entirely out of line," she scolded him when they were back in his Camero and headed home along Morris Munger Road.

"I can't stand your fake friends," he said. "Money does not impress me."

"Good, because you'll never have any if you keep working at the garage." Kim removed the engagement ring from her finger and dramatically dropped it in the cup holder. "Until you grow up, we can't plan a future together."

"You don't want to marry me?"

"I don't want to marry an immature boy," Kim said. "You once told me that I make you a better man. But I don't see any evidence of that. We just keep going round and round in circles. It's infuriating!"

"It's infuriating, is it?" Ross was yelling now. "Infuriating?"

He took the curve along the road a little too sharp, and the Camero skidded across the lanes almost hitting an abandoned fruit stand. Slamming on the brakes, he skidded onto the gravel shoulder. In one angry swoop, he grabbed the diamond ring from the cup holder, rolled down the window and chucked it outside.

Kim screamed at him and jumped out the Camero. Running into the road, she searched for the ring as cars around her skidded and stopped. Horns blared and one angry driver shouted and shook his fist at her. Kim ignored them all, frantically searching for that elegant Solitaire diamond ring with a thin, two-toned band.

But she couldn't find it.

Crying and standing in the middle of the road, she lifted her head to see Ross roll-up his window and skid back onto the pavement. The tires spun loudly, before the old Camero sped off down the highway.

It would be the last time she ever saw him.

That night, she walked home, alone, hoping he would be there waiting for her. Hoping he had cooled off. But the townhouse was empty, save for Zeus watching for her out the front bay window. Ross though wasn't anywhere to be found.

A week later, she was still angry and boxed up many of his things. She had Mallory drive her to Eddy's Garage downtown and placed the box outside his locker. To teach him a lesson. But he wasn't there either. And if he ever got the box, she never knew. He never responded to the gesture.

As the days passed, Kim found herself drawn to Morris Munger Road. There, she searched for that diamond ring. Sometimes she wondered if Ross backtracked to the spot and beat her to it. Maybe he knew exactly where he threw it and had already returned to retrieve it. Since she didn't know for sure, she continued looking.

Everyone thought she was crazy for being so persistent. "It's in the past," Mallory would say. "Get over him." But she couldn't. She even heard the neighbors and the landlord asking Mallory what she was doing on the side of the road.

"What's she looking for?" Mrs. Roundtree asked. "Again and again she searches that road. She's driving herself crazy."

"I think that boy really hurt her," the landlord added when Mallory told him that Ross had tossed her engagement ring out the car window. "He didn't deserve her."

"I'm just glad Ross is finally out of her life," Mallory would tell them. "Good riddance and I hope she never speaks to him again."

Now, after five weeks, she _was_ about to see him again.

* * * * * * *

She had so much to say. It was all she had really thought about. But now she was unsure of herself and her future. So she did the only thing she could: concentrate on the old downtown buildings rushing past her outside the passenger-side window.

"For Ross' sake, I hope he's a gentleman and apologizes to you," Mallory finally said, breaking the silence. She reached over to Kim and took her hand. Kim turned her head and Mallory winked at her. "Else when I get through with him, he's going to be missing enough body parts to qualify for handicapped parking."

Mallory laughed at her threat as she pulled onto Eighth Street and into Eddy's Garage on the corner of Cypress. Kim and Mallory got out of the Miata as a young mechanic with greasy blonde hair and wearing a black sleeveless Metallica t-shirt approached them.

"You broads needing your oil changed?" he asked, shooting them a toothy grin and wiping his hands on a rag. "It's Wednesday. We got a Ladies Special running on Wednesdays."

"No, thank you." Kim looked past him into the garage. She ran her hands along her sides down to her upper thigh, as if to smooth out the wrinkles of her tight red dress. She thought there would be more men standing around with tools, working on cars. "I'm looking for someone," she said, then added, "Ross McGuire."

The young man looked puzzled. "Who?"

"Ross McGuire?" Kim repeated. "Tall, nice build, works out, early twenties with short black hair."

He gave her a blank stare. Kim laughed and glanced at Mallory and then back at the mechanic.

"Ross McGuire," she said louder, a little more forceful. "He's worked here for about a year."

The mechanic, either bored with the conversation or thinking Kim was hallucinating, shrugged his shoulders.

"I ain't never seen a guy like that before, but I just started."

Kim bit her lower lip, glancing around the garage. "Where's the owner, Ed? Do you know him?"

He pointed to the office in back. Kim and Mallory walked toward it.

Ed looked up from behind a cluttered desk as the girls approached. He was a middle aged business man wearing jeans and a dirty Guns-N-Roses t-shirt.

"Miss Bradford," he said. "How are ya?"

"Fine Ed. How've you been?" She held out her hand. He grasped it and shook it, then released her to swipe away the beads of sweat on his forehead.

"What can I do for you?"

"I'm looking for Ross."

"Ain't seen him for a couple of weeks now."

"Really?" This surprised her. "Where'd he go?"

"He'd been threat'n to head on outta here. I kinda figured he finally walked."

"He didn't say where he was going? Another job?" Her voice raised an octave from a little bit of excitement mixed with panic. "Did he get the box I left him?"

"You didn't know?" Ed squinted. "He jest didn't show up one night a couple a weeks back. You ain't seen 'em?"

"We had a fight and he left me. I broke off our engagement," she said quietly. "I hadn't realized he'd quit his job too."

"It ain't suprisin', Kim. Ross din just have a chip on his shoulder... he had a whole boulder. His attitude was tough as hell to handle sometimes."

"I see.." Kim shrugged, glancing at Mallory,

then turned. She started to leave when Ed called to her again.

"Hey Kim. You know what," he started, getting up from his desk. "Someone else was looking for him too."

"Really?" She turned back around. "Who?"

"Some guy, a kid about your age," he said.

"Who was it? Do you remember his name?"

"Naw..." Ed shook his head. "But he said he goes to the University. He was a thin, little guy with black hair with heavy bangs that fell into his face. Maybe you know him?"

Kim inhaled deeply, thinking about her literature class.

* * * * * * *

At that same moment, a black and white patrol car rolled down the muddy road behind the Flying J Truck Stop, finally parking behind a 1987 midnight blue Camero. The officer stepped out, moved cautiously toward the Camero, and peered through the black tinted windows. The vehicle had been reported abandoned and left by the roadside. But he saw nothing unusual. The front seats were worn and beer cans piled in the floor board. The keys were left in the ignition. He paused, and briefly scanned the woods around the car. Nothing unusual.

Returning to the patrol car, he radioed dispatch. "We have an abandoned 1987 Camero. Dark blue. License plate number X13-78G." A voice answered, crackling over the radio. "Vehicle is registered to a

Ross McGuire at 1200 Meadowbrooke Lane..."
    Writing out a ticket, he got back out of the squad car and returned to the Camero, placing the ticket behind a windshield wiper.

9
Deadly Still Waters

Thursday, January 13, 2000
10:38 AM

The Professor droned on in front of a classroom of roughly eighty students. Kim's mind was elsewhere. She made notes in her spiral notebook, writing, *If you forget me, there's something I want you to know.* She thought of Ross, and the poems he had written. The beautiful, handwritten love letters.

Earlier, she had walked to the University taking the longer route along Morris Munger Road. Just as she had done for the last five weeks, she stopped at the curve in the road and searched the ground around the old fruit stand and real estate sign. She searched for the ring, but still didn't find it.

Five weeks, three days and seven hours, she thought. *Five weeks, three days and seven hours.*

Then the warm memory turned cold. Once again she could feel him watching. Feel his eyes burning holes in the back of her head. Self-consciously, she looked up and behind her.

There was a classroom of students around her, but she made eye contact with the black haired boy in the back. He was glaring at her again.

Kim had tried to approach him before class. She had even arrived early and waited for him. But class started and the Professor began his lecture when the kid slinked through the doors. He was now sitting in the back of the classroom. After watching him a moment, she looked back down at the notes. She had been scribbling the romantic phrase, *"If you forget me."* The Professor suddenly stopped talking and the classroom went silent. Kim turned around.

"If we're not disturbing you, Miss Bradford," he said. He started to continue his lecture when Kim raised her hand, interrupting him.

The Professor called on her again and she asked about the poem, If You Forget Me. "What does it mean?"

"Neruda," he said. "It's his most famous poem."

"It's about unrequited love?" Kim asked. "It's so sad, though. Why would someone in love give this poem to, say, his girlfriend?"

The Professor put a hand to his bearded chin and turned, as if contemplating the question.

"I cannot be sure without talking to Neruda himself, and of course that is impossible since he is dead now these thirty years." He laughed as if he had made a joke. The class was silent. "But as I reread this poem, it occurs to me that it is not so much selfish, 'Hey, stop loving me and I'll stop loving you.

116

Easy breasy.' No, this love he talks about is too expansive to drop so easily as if costing nothing. You can hear it in the lines, 'Everything carries me to you / as if everything that exists."

He moved toward Kimberly, sitting in the middle of the classroom. He continued.

"Instead, I think this is a poem about how love cannot exist in and of itself. Love needs love. If one stops loving you, it is not a law of physics that you will stop loving them back, but they should not be surprised if they too are forgotten and replaced with another love."

He picked up the poetry book on Kim's desk and studied it a moment. It looked like he was reading the handwritten inscription inside the front cover. He set it back down.

"This poem is a warning to his lover that she could lose *his* love if she's not careful," he said to Kim, almost as if she was the only student in the classroom. "This poem tells me to be careful. In fact, Neruda says things like, 'Everything carries me to you,' and 'My love feeds on your love,' which tells me that he is admitting his dependence on her. Thus if she stops loving him and forgets him, his love will likewise diminish."

The student in the back of the class shuffled in his seat. "All I see in this poem is a cynic who loves only for the sake of getting love in return," he said.

All heads in the classroom turned to him. It was the thin, quiet boy with shaggy black hair that fell down into his face. He pushed the hair out of his eyes and glanced at Kim. Their eyes met. He glared at her, as if angry that she even brought it up.

"Michael, that is so provocative," the professor

said, leaving the silent exchange between his two students unacknowledged. "Would you care to elaborate?"

The boy's eyes widened as tense lines formed on his face. The muscles on his forearm hardened. After gulping a deep breath, he finally spoke.

"Well, if his partner's love for him diminishes, he mercilessly abandons her." The boy shifted in his seat and his voice squeaked. "What a horribly self-centered person he is. He should not be given the right to love anyone. He is a disgrace for all the pure hearted lovers in this world."

The class was silent.

"I must admit I'm more than a little surprised," the Professor said, slowly. "You're generally so quiet and reserved. I don't think you've said two words all year."

The boy looked down. "Still waters run deep."

After class, the boy collected his books and made his way out of the classroom. Kim jumped from her desk and ran after him.

"Wait," she yelled at the edge of the door. In the hallway, he stopped and turned around to face her. Other students pushed past them as they blocked the door.

"Did you go to Eddy's Garage looking for my fiancée?" Kim asked hesitantly.

He didn't answer. After several seconds of awkward silence, she continued.

"Okay..." She forced forward, closer to him as the last student lumbered out of the classroom and bumped into her. She glanced at the clumsy girl, then back at him. "So why were you there? Looking for my fiancée?"

He sheepishly paused and looked down at his feet. Exasperated, Kim gave up. She moved past him and started down the hallway. He called after her.

"Wait. My name is Michael."

Kim stopped walking. She turned her head and gave him a sidelong glance. "Hello, Michael."

"Hello." His face closed, as if her was guarding a secret.

"I'm Kim." She walked back to him, standing shoulder to shoulder. She held her breath, waiting, then forced a thin smile. "So, are you going to tell me why you were looking for my fiancée at Eddy's Garage?"

He shook his head, but said nothing. Silence grew tight with tension. The smile left her face and Kim told him she had to go.

"Wait!" he called out again. "Have you seen him? I mean, have you heard anything... from Ross, I mean."

"Yes..." she thought about it a moment before saying more. It would be the first time she told anyone. She drew her lips in thoughtfully. "We have dinner plans on Friday."

"Oh." He stared. It was as if she just slapped him. The tension between them increased with frightening intensity, then his expression darkened with an unreadable emotion.

Kim took a step back. Stumbling ever so slightly, she apologized, then said she really had to go. Turning, she walked away, picking up pace.

Later that afternoon, Kim tried to disguise her foul mood when she walked into the old folks home. Nurse Carla was helping a man walk along the wall, his hands gripping the railing. Seeing her, Carla lifted up and beamed.

"Miss Bradford, your Grandaddy seems to be feeling better today." She waved a hand, motioning Kim to come closer. "I took him to the cafeteria to eat his peas and carrots and then we went for a walk."

"He's out of his room?"

"He's in the rec room talking to all the pretty ladies." Nurse Carla laughed. "An' child, he's been there all morning."

Kim turned down the opposite hallway and made her way past a pair of elderly women in a walker and wheel chair. There was a woman in a nightgown sitting in a gray folding chair outside her room. She called out to Kim with her arms raised, asking if she'd seen her little daffodil. Kim made her way past them to the Rec Room at the end of the wing.

Across from the kitchen, the Rec Room was a large den with metal fold-out chairs and tables. There was a piano in the corner. Several television were pushed against opposite walls with couches positioned in front of them. There were about thirty patients in the room. Some were in groups, sitting at tables where board games were laid out. There were two catatonic men staring at a television set.

Kim found her Grandfather, dressed and wearing a brown sweater, sitting in an arm chair along the back wall. He was facing a picturesque window that looked down at the street.

She walked over to him, placing a hand on his shoulder. He was asleep in the armchair, his body slightly leaning toward the left. Quietly snoring, he had been staring out the window, watching the world below him. Kim knelt beside him.

"Hi, Grampa." She paused. Feeling a cool draft coming from the window pane, she fixed his sweater so it better covered his chest and neck. She thought about returning to his room to retrieve the old quilt, but changed her mind. It would probably get left behind or someone would take it. Then she straightened up and sat in a matching armchair beside him.

"You look good today." She watched him a moment. His head leaning to the side, he was breathing deeply, snoring with several light wheezes followed by one long sigh. Then it all started over again. "I love you, Grampa," she said into his ear.

She said nothing more to him during this visit. She just simply sat beside him and watched him sleep in the chair.

* * * * * * *

In her bedroom loft, Mallory lay on her stomach atop the bed. Her legs bent upwards and a single high heeled shoe dangled from her left foot. With one hand, her fingers pressed the buttons on her phone as she held the receiver between her shoulder and chin. She groaned at the shrill beep of a busy signal, hung up and dialed again.

It was another KYGL radio contest: The thirty-fifth caller would win $3,500. She was caller number seventeen, then caller number forty-six. Frustrated she slammed down the receiver.

When the doorbell rang, her mood seemed suddenly buoyant again. Leaping off the bed, she yelled, "Just a minute!" and scrambled downstairs.

Mallory signed for the UPS package at the door, then tore it open. Beneath sheets of bubble wrap, she found a black sniper rifle, and a red polished DM13, and a shiny, black Tippmann X7 Phenum Electropneumatic paintball marker. She reached in the box and lifted out a red and pink assault matrix.

There was a note attached that read,

> *"Mallory,*
> *I picked out these DAM's especially for you.*
> *Please share these with Kimberly and I'm*
> *looking forward to seeing you both this*
> *weekend.*
> *— Dr. Alec Whitman.*
>
> *P.S. I've included two tickets to the game this*
> *afternoon. Hope you both can make it."*

Mallory put down the handwritten note and peered back into the box. She found an envelope with two tickets for this evening's charity exhibition game with the Tampa Yankees--- a solid two months before Spring Training. It was the majors versus the minors in a winter game benefitting St. Jude's Children's Cancer Center.

Her smile broadened with approval. Gunz Gonzales would be there. Now she had to get Kim there.

From her upstairs bedroom window, Mallory watched for her best friend. When she finally saw Kim walk through the security gates and cross the parking lot, she glanced back at the box of paint guns.

With the sense of conviction that was part of her character, she stood and backed away from the window. It was time for her to go to work.

* * * * * * *

Zeus greeted Kim at the front door when she stepped inside and walked through the living room. She threw her literature books on the kitchen table. She held the poetry book for a moment, then threw that down as well and moved back to the living room. Zeus followed.

Picking up the phone on the end table next to the recliner, Kim dialed Ross' mother.

"Mrs. McGuire," she said, when a woman answered on the other end. It was Ross' mother. "This is Kimberly. Have you seen Ross?"

"Not in the last few hours." The woman's voice chuckled, as if she was joking. Kim knew though that if she read between the lines, she'd find his mother was deadly serious.

"So is he there?" Kim asked impatiently. "Did he go home?"

"He's not here. I haven't seen either of you since Christmas, you know. You'd think a boy would visit or at least call his Mama once in a while."

"When did you last talk to him?"

"I told you --- last Christmas. And even then it was just a phone call. No card or visit, just a quick phone call," she rambled. A twinge of anger rose in her voice, then she broke off midsentence. Her tone changed. *"Is something the matter?"*

"He quit his job."

"Well he's always quitting something. Am I right?"

"But did he tell you that we broke up?"

The mother laughed. *"Again, he's always quitting something. He gets that from his father's side, you know."*

Kim thanked her, hung up the phone then plopped down onto the old recliner. She picked up the scrapbook and flipped through the pages. Not really looking at any specific picture, she just retreated into the memories. Finally, she read Ross' poem again.

> *"Oh, Love rips the heart in pieces,*
> > *When distance fills the empty creases*
> > *Of time*
> *And days become long stretches*
> > *Of pain and wretches*
> > *Of torment*
> > > *When our love ceases."*

That little pang deep in her temple returned, and instinctively she knew something was wrong. Something was terribly wrong, even if she didn't want to admit it. A clang at the front door startled her, as the door swung open and Mallory bound into the living room, dressed in fatigues and carrying the large box of plastic guns. The exhibition ticketswere in her pocket.

"Taaaaa - daaa!" she exclaimed, posing in the doorway. Setting down the box, she held up the pink rifle. "Come on, make my day!"

"You look like you've been drafted," Kim laughed. The green-black-brown fatigues drooped on her like an ill-fitting sweat suit and the combat boots made her feet look three times larger. It was certainly a fashion statement. "What's going on?"

"It's for our paintball weekend." She put down the pink gun and opened the box. "There's a Tippmann X7 Phenum Electropneumatic paintball marker. That's yours."

Kim moved toward her. "What are these?"

"Paint ball guns," she explained. "They shoot paint balls, or pellets really. They're for our warrior weekend on Saturday."

"I'm not going," Kim said flatly and turned back toward the kitchen. "I'll be busy."

"Doing what?" Mallory followed her with interest. Pausing, she glanced at the scrapbook in Kim's hands. Setting down the box of plastic guns, she walked over to Kim and took the black scrapbook from her hands. "I thought you got rid of everything that belonged to him."

"Not everything," Kim said quietly. She watched Mallory flip through the pages, her eyes widening.

"These are love letters..." Mallory turned another page and found the poem Kim most treasured. She read it out loud. "Oh, love rips the heart in pieces and distance fills the empty creases. Ross wrote this?"

"Yes, for me." Kim walked over to the table and picked up the Pablo Neruda poetry book. She handed it to Mallory. It was time she told her everything. "And he gave me this."

Mallory took the poetry book and opened the cover. She read the inscription out loud.

"For my Darling Bonnie. You will always be my angel. Love, Daddy." Mallory flipped through the pages, glancing at the poems. "Who's Bonnie?"

"I don't know."

"And Ross gave this to you?"

"Yes, earlier this week..." Kim said.

Mallory shut the book. "He gave you this book, this week?"

"Yes... along with a note to meet him on Friday night," she said quietly. Zeus whimpered at her feet. She glanced at him, then back at Mallory. "I was going to tell you."

"Oh, sweetie. Something isn't right here," Mallory's tone was chiding as she studied the invitation. A look of alarm flushed over her face, but Kim ignored it.

"It's romantic," she insisted.

"Yeah, real romantic." Mallory flipped the invitation over to see if anything was written on the back. "Why's he being so elusive? Why not just call you and say, *hey, we need to talk*?"

"It's his way. He's poetic and passionate and quiet," she said, then thought back to what Michael had said in class earlier. "Still waters run deep."

"*Deadly* still waters," Mallory added. "I just don't like this."

Tossing the invitation aside, she showed Kim

the tickets to the charity baseball game. She was deliberately changing the subject from Ross, which Kim didn't particularly like.

"I don't know." Kim took the two tickets from Mallory's hand and studied them. "A baseball game in the winter?"

"For little sick kids," Mallory explained. "It's a good cause."

"But baseball, in January?" Kim asked again, trying to get her head wrapped around the idea. "Only in Florida…"

"Come on. Besides, Gunz Gonzales is playing in it," Mallory gushed.

Upstairs in Kim's bedroom loft, Mallory slipped out of the fatigues and found the white chiffon cocktail dress still hanging in the small, organized closet. It looked more like a slip really, and Mallory smiled when she saw it. Kim shook her head.

"You can't wear that to a baseball game."

"I'm not wearing it for the game; I'm wearing it for Gunz." Mallory slipped into the skimpy white dress. Practically see-through, it clung provocatively to her body and left nothing to the imagination. "I want him to see me in this dress."

"Everyone's going to see you in that dress," Kim said with a not-so-subtle hint of disapproval. "There's going to be families and sick kids there."

"It's Chanel."

"It's a charity afternoon baseball game." Kim took a pair of jeans from a middle drawer in her dresser and handed them toward her. Mallory scoffed at this, but relented. She flipped the straps off her shoulders and let the dress fall to her ankles. She then lovingly picked it back up and returned it to the hanger in the closet. She sighed. Stepping into tight jeans and white tennis shoes, Mallory finally wrapped a checkered scarf over her red hair.

"You know we're not going to watch baseball, don't you?" Mallory asked.

"I hate it when you do this to me. I don't want to be set-up."

"A set-up?" Mallory asked with a slight smile of smug delight. "Whatever do you mean?"

"Am I going to run into the old head shrink at this charity exhibition game?"

"He's a psychiatrist *and* he's a rich doctor." Mallory's eyes sharpened as she quite openly appraised Kim, perhaps wondering if all the energy and effort was actually worth it. "Who do you think gave me the tickets?"

"I'm going, but just so you know, this doesn't change anything," Kim said. "Absolutely nothing will happen between the old shrink and me. I'm still meeting Ross on Friday night."

"I know," Mallory said. "Even if it kills you..."

Shaking her head and resigning to her fate, Kimberly followed Mallory into the parking lot and into her freshly waxed Miata. A moment later, they pulled out and sped down the street.

Behind them, the headlights of a red BMW flipped on. The driver revved the engine, then tore down the street after them.

10

Field of Prey

Driving south on Interstate 75, the girls headed toward Tampa. It was a good hour on the road, and Mallory punched up KYGL, got Ricky Martin playing "Livin' la Vida Loca." She adjusted the bass to just where she could see the dashboard vibrate, and drummed on the steering wheel.

"I'm so excited that you're finally going to meet the rich doctor," she said.

"The old shrink?" Kim asked, sitting beside her. Reaching out, she turned the radio knob, lowering the volume. "And you know this isn't going to go anywhere."

"The doctor's a catch," Mallory insisted. "And I hope after meeting him, you'll see that and blow off meeting Ross tomorrow night."

"Not going to happen," Kim didn't care if Mallory approved or not, and made that very clear in her voice. "I just think this is the first step in the right direction."

"Maybe. Maybe not. I don't know what to think," Mallory said slowly, as if taken back by Kim's sudden forcefulness. Pausing, she glanced at Kim then added, "But I do know that Ross shouldn't have been at the New Year's Eve party that night and now, in light of everything that's happened, you need to put as much distance between you and him as possible."

"Mal, you're one to talk."

Coming to an exit ramp, Mallory turned her Miata off the Interstate. She pulled into the Flying J Truckstop and up to a gas pump. Both girls climbed out of the car, and Mallory continued the conversation outside.

"Are you even certain it's Ross who set this up?" she asked. She swiped her credit card at the pump, selected a grade of gas and then removed the hose and nozzle.

"Of course it was. Who else would it be?" Kim glanced at the convenience store, and the small phone booth just beyond the parking lot. There was yellow police tape barricading it from the public. Behind it, along the dirt road running behind the store through the miles of woodlands and cow pastures, two police cars were parked with their lights flashing. Kim wondered what was going on.

Mallory shook her head. "If it's Ross, then why all the theatrics? Why is he sending you a book of morbid poetry? Why pass you cryptic notes?"

Kim wasn't listening. She was focused on the murky woods, and then the empty phone booth. Several police officers appeared to be combing the area. Then a semi truck pulled into the parking lot, grumbling loudly as it rolled past, blocking her view.

Mallory finished pumping gas and replaced the lever in the pump. She was still talking, apparently unaware that Kim wasn't even listening. "So, why meet you on Friday? Why not tonight? Or last night?" she asked, getting back into the car. "Or at the New Year's Eve party?"

The questions remained unanswered as the girls left the gas station and headed back to the Interstate.

Three thousand people filled Steinbrenner Field in Tampa. The crowd paraded from the parking lot to the ticket booths to the stadium entrance gates, with flags rippling in a chilly northern wind. Among children's sneaker feet running, the crunch of nacho chewing, the monotonous calling of a program vendor, the collective chuckling of people standing in hot dog lines, Mallory led Kim to the outfield seats.

"There he is," she said, pointing. Dr. Alec Whitman was hanging over the outfield railing before batting practice. Behind him on the field, the players were out limbering up. Mallory gushed. "Doesn't he look dreamy?"

Turning to them, the doctor smiled. He was average height, just under six feet, wearing a turquoise and black bowling shirt and tan shorts. His hair was an odd shade of orangey-brown, with a little twinge of gray.

"Kimberly Bradford," he said, approaching them with his hand extended. "Pleased to finally meet you. I'm Dr. Alec Whitman."

"Good to meet you too." Kim took his hand and lightly shook it, staring at his hair.

Mallory was staring at it too, as if trying to figure out exactly what to say. He held up his arms, offering a hug. She embraced him and pecked his cheek, then stepped back.

"What's going on here?" she asked, motioning to his head.

Dr. Whitman smiled. He ran a hand through his full head of orangey-brown hair. "It's called Indian Summer," he said. "You like it?"

"You colored your hair," she said through clenched teeth. "Don't you just look delicious."

As Mallory quietly apologized to Kim, they found their seats in the bleachers. Kim glared at Mallory then moved to the seat beside the psychiatrist. Mallory sat to her right. After a short ceremony with a giant cardboard check for the St. Jude's Children's Cancer Research Center, and a rendition of The Star Spangled Banner sung by the local high school choir, the first pitch was thrown.

Mallory searched for Gunz, and found him warming up, in the on deck circle, rotating his shoulders, twisting his torso. She called out to him and he looked over his shoulder at Mallory and Kim in the stands for a moment. He tipped his cap, then returned to his practice swing.

Mallory grabbed Kim and waved.

The crowd cheered each hitter, especially Gunz Gonzales, who hammed it up in his bright white jersey. A group of fanatical middle-aged women held up signs reading "Grease it Gunz!" and "Gunz Got Game!" A lone voice in the outfield, faraway but still booming, cried out, "Guunnnnzzzoooo!"

Dr. Whitman paid no attention to the batter,

seemingly focused on the girls. Leaning over Kim to address Mallory, he said, "I trust that you received my gift."

Mallory laughed. "The box of red and pink assault rifles? I love them!"

A sigh of relief broke from his lips, and he ran a hand through his hair again. It left a streak of orange on his palm "They shoot pink paint pellets, so our adversaries are going to look mighty pretty all splattered up in dye." He laughed as if he had just made a joke, then noticed the orange stain on his right hand. He quickly moved it to his lap and hid it under his left hand. Then he turned his head to speak into Kim's ear.

"Me and these college kids, we do this kind of thing all the time," he bragged, almost as if he was trying to prove his youth. "So feel free to pick anything out."

Kim glared at Mallory. "We haven't decided whether or not we're going."

"I decided for both of us," Mallory corrected her. "We're going."

"I have to check my calendar."

Mallory wasn't listening. "I've already RSVP'd."

"Mal, this is infuriating. You know how important Friday night is to me. And if everything goes well, I should be preoccupied for the entire weekend…"

The doctor cleared his throat. "Am I interrupting something?"

Kim glanced at him a moment then started to get up, saying she was getting a hot dog. Mallory grabbed her arm and forced her back into her seat.

"You're going to miss the game," she said.

On the field, a fastball ignited like a flash toward

Gunz's bat. He swung. The ball cracked wood, skidding hard toward third. Mallory's body tensed. Kim moved toward the edge of her seat, as did the doctor next to her. They watched Gunz run to first. It looked as though the shortstop would get to the ball on third. Seconds later, the ball slid under his glove, into the outfield. Gunz scored, bringing in two runners. The crowd cheered.

"That's my lover boy!" Mallory screamed, rising from her seat.

New York scored another in the first inning, but so did Tampa. And Tampa scored again in the third with bloop singles and an error by the pitcher.

Despite the excitement, things didn't seem to be going the way Mallory had planned between Kim and the Doctor. She grimaced at this. Finally stretching over Kim, Mallory placed a hand on the Doctor's knee. "So tell Kim about your practice," she said. "I bet you have some interesting stories to tell."

"A few." He was obviously trying not to sound too pretentious. "But I have been on manic depressive overloads lately."

Mallory threw her head back, laughing at his joke. Then she tagged Kim's shoulder. "Did you hear that, Kim?"

"Yes, manic depressive overloads. I'm sitting right next to him," she answered. She noticed the sweat on his forehead was causing the hair color to run, creating an orange smudge along his hair line. Kim's eyes widened and she looked over at Mallory, glancing toward his head, seeing if her friend saw this too. Mallory ignored it and reached over her again, taking the Doctor's hand.

"I just think it would be fun to have access to all

that secret, personal information," she said. "Come on, Doctor, tell us some of your most warped cases and let me try to figure out who they are."

"No." The Doctor shook his head. "You know, I can't talk about my patients."

"There's some pretty sick tickets living in Stillwater."

"I will give you that," he said thoughtfully. Mallory released his hand, and he folded it in his lap. "Since the murder of the Congressman, the number of mental medical emergencies has increased tenfold."

"So, so sad," Mallory let out a loud, audible sigh, leaned back into her seat. There was a streak of orange on her fingers and studied it as she spoke. "And that's why you missed connecting with my friend here for lunch the other day."

"And New Year's Eve," Kim added. "He stood me up twice. Two times. In a row."

"I know I owe you an apology," the Doctor said. "But Mallory's right, I have been working with a particularly disturbed patient lately who has monopolized a great deal of my time."

"This is the patient who was upset about the Congressman's murder?" Kim asked.

He smiled. "Did Addison tell you that?"

"Yes." Kim took a breath and thought about Addison's story from the other day at the diner. "That and that the Congressman's murder is connected to another murder that occurred back in the Seventies."

"The Congressman's brother was murdered 25 years ago," he explained. "But that's not where it ends. There's a gruesome, violent connection."

Kim leaned forward. "What do you mean?"

"The teenage boy who was killed, the Congressman's brother," he started, "when they found his body the police revealed that someone had driven some kind of spike through his right eye. As if it were a lobotomy gone wrong."

Kim and Mallory shrunk back at the same time. The doctor continued.

"The Congressman was found in that exact condition," he said, leaning forward. The orange smudges along his hairline were expanding. He made a slashing motion with his hand. "They used the ice pick method."

"What's that?" Kim asked, staring at his forehead. He smiled and raised a hand, bringing it toward Kim's face. His fingers were orange.

"It's when a doctor inserts a thin, metal pipette into the orbital frontal cortex and enters the soft tissue of the frontal lobe." The doctor's hand moved toward her eye and he drew a hypothetical line along the side of her nose up toward her eyebrow. "A few simple, smooth, up and down jerks to sever the lateral hypothalamus," he continued. "All resulting in an immediate reduction of stress for our disturbed patient."

Kim swiped his hand away. She could smell the hair dye. "Are you saying someone tried to lobotomize the Congressman?"

"I'm saying, if it was, it was a botched lobotomy from some kind of mad scientist. Both brothers died the same way."

"How could you possibly know that?" Kim stared at him, struggle for words. "I haven't read anything like that in the papers."

"I have a friend on the police force," he explained. "They consult me as I'm a psychiatrist working with…" The doctor paused; he smiled at Mallory. "Some pretty sick tickets living in Stillwater."

Kim looked at Mallory. Mallory looked at her, then back at the Doctor.

"Kim's right about the paint ball weekend," she said quickly. "We haven't decided if we're going yet or not. We'll let you know…"

The seventh inning stretch came with a lot of hubbub from the loud speakers and overhead monitors. On the field, there were a few hits that didn't amount to much, and then Guns was warming up in the on deck circle again.

This didn't escape Mallory's attention either.

"You're the best, Lover Boy," she yelled to him, and in a movement so small but so big he turned, smiled, and nodded to her, in front of the entire crowd. His gesture was caught on the jumbo-tron for everyone to see.

Unfortunately, this time he struck out.

As the team ran back to the dugout, Kim and Mallory got up out of their seats, left the Doctor alone and headed to the ladies room.

"This is the worst set-up ever," Kim said. Near the concession stand underneath bleachers, they waited in line. "I'm never letting you live this one down."

"He's just trying to look hip and young."
Kim noted both derision and sympathy mingled in Mallory's glance. She started to protest, but was interrupted when a man called out to them. Turning, she saw him push his way through the crowd.

The man waved and yelled Mallory's name.

"Addison?" Mallory stuttered, surprised. He was wearing a suit and tie with a baseball cap. She almost didn't recognize him. "Addison, what are you doing here?"

11
Final Inning

"I've been looking for you," Addison said, out of breath. He looked oddly out of place, wearing a suit and tie with a baseball cap on his head. "I've been looking for you everywhere."

He glanced at Kim, then studied Mallory. They were standing in line for the ladies restroom and he stepped in line with them. "Doctor Whitman said he was escorting the two of you to this exhibition charity baseball game."

"You came all the way out to Tampa?" Mallory touched his arm. "Is everything alright?"

He shrugged, as if questioning whether or not he heard her correctly. Reaching out, he took hold of her hand. "I have some news to tell you. Bad news, I'm afraid."

"Pudd'n Toes… No!" A glazed look of despair spread over her face. "What is it?"

JC Gatlin

"I'm afraid I will have to go out of town for a few days." He gripped her hand. "On business."

Mallory's face scrunched as if she was concentrating to understand.

"You drove all the way out here to tell me you were leaving town for a few days?" she asked. "Pudd'n Toes, please. If I didn't know better, I'd think you were a stalker."

"I'm headed to the airport right now and I'm in a fantastic hurry," he said. "And I didn't want you to worry that I was missing."

Mallory laughed, as if suddenly understanding. She glanced at Kim then turned back to him.

"Because of Ross," she said with unwelcome frankness. "You didn't want me to think you'd disappeared on me like Ross did to Kim."

Kim sighed as the line moved forward. It was their turn next. Addison continued. "But I can cancel my plans if you'd rather I stay close by... in case something happens."

Kim looked up as Mallory laughed.

"Get out of here." Mallory laughed and gently pushed him. It was their turn to walk into the ladies restroom and they were now holding up the line. They stepped forward as she continued talking. "We can manage on our own."

"I just don't want to leave you girls alone." He grabbed her hand, holding her back. Sudden anger lit his eyes. "And you are alone, right?"

Mallory laughed again and pulled her hand from his grip. "I swear you say the oddest things some times."

An awkward pause grew tight with tension until Mallory finally wrapped her arms around him.

140

"Everything will be fine. We'll see you when you get back." She brushed his beard with her fingers, her breath hot in his ear. "My credit card payment is past due…"

"I'll mail them a check." He smiled and winked.

With that, Kim and Mallory disappeared into the restroom. Addison stood watching them a moment, when his cellular phone buzzed inside his breast pocket. He removed it from his jacket and flipped it open.

"Hello," he answered, then turned back toward the entrance. Carrying on a conversation, he tossed his ticket into a metal garbage can and left the stadium.

The bottom of the ninth ushered in and Kim, distracted, didn't even realize it until she asked, "Wait, is this the last inning?"

"They're quarters," Mallory corrected her, shaking her head in mock embarrassment.

They were back in their seats again, and this time Mallory was sitting in the middle between Kim and Dr. Whitman. In response to Kim's question, he said, more sighed, "Not if they don't score. They're tied." Then he motioned to Mallory. "Gunz is up this inning."

Mallory leaned forward and looked out onto the field. The game was tied. The bases were loaded. This was actually kind of exciting.

Gunz stepped up to home plate, beginning a ritual that all fans knew well. Feet spread, he leaned back on his hips, rotated to his left a couple of times, then to his right. Loosened his shoulders. He tapped

his bat on the edge of the plate, settled in, and
Mallory rose. The stadium was silent.

A young, unknown closer for Tampa stared him
down, wound up, threw.

It was a good pitch. Gunz leaned back. Swung.
CRACK! Every head in the stadium raised, following
the ball as it shot out of the park.

Cheers erupted in the stadium. It brought every
player off the bench and they swarmed the field.
Children from the cancer center rushed out, and they
jumped, hugged and high-fived one another at the
mound with the athletes.

The Doctor thanked the girls for a wonderful
afternoon and invited them to get drinks with him. His
hair dye was now running down in orange streaks
along his forehead and neck. The girls couldn't take
their eyes off it. Mallory declined his offer, as she and
Kim were escorted into the club house as special
guests of Gunz Gonzales.

In the clubhouse, surrounded by a celebrating
team, Kim and Mallory found Gunz. He greeted the
girls and his jersey was unbuttoned and open,
showing off his pectoral muscles.

"I told you I should've worn the chiffon," Mallory
said to Kim. After thirty minutes, she tossed Kim the
keys to her Miata.

"Gunz is taking me into downtown Tampa
tonight," she said with a wink.

Kim drove Mallory's little Mazda Miata home in
the early setting darkness of winter. As expected, she
could see Zeus in the front bay window, staring
intently out the glass, waiting for her to return. He

barked as she entered the townhome. Zeus was excited to see her, and Kim fed him and took him outside.

Mrs. Roundtree was walking Little Rosie, her Pekingese, at the same time, and Zeus lit up in a terror, threatening to eat the little dog. Rosie yelped back, tugging on her leash. Mrs. Roundtree had to pick the little fur ball up in her arms as Kim struggled to hold back Zeus.

"That dog needs tranquilizers," she said to Kim, wagging a finger on her free hand. "Because of that militarized attack dog, the landlord is thinking about adding a no pets clause to all our leases."

"I heard," Kim said as she yanked Zeus back with all her might. She was tugging him across the lawn back toward her townhome just as the phone was ringing.

Kim could hear the urgent *brrrrrrng-brrrrrrng-brrrrrrng* from the parking lot, and rushed inside to answer it. Curious and excited now, Zeus followed. Collapsing into the old recliner in the living room, she reached for the receiver. "Hello?"

There was no answer. Only breathing.

"Is someone there?"

A quiet, masculine voice murmured another Pablo Neruda poem across the line. He read it with a blistering fervor. His voice swelled with an urgent passion that left Kim breathless. Static crackled again, then the line went silent.

"Ross... Are you still there?"

He didn't answer, but she could hear him breathing.

Rising out of the recliner, she carried the phone to the front door, its black cord stretching across the living room. Listening to the breathing on the other end, Kim shut and locked the door.

She then moved to the front bay window and peeked outside. The moon had long since vanished and the night sky was uncharacteristically black and forbidding; an angry wind howled and rattled the glass. She paid no attention to it as she stared out into the dark parking lot. There, she noticed it.

A red BMW.

There were no lights. The car was not running. But someone was sitting in the driver's seat, watching her.

Addison Gaynor, she thought.

"Are you still there?" Her voice drifted into a hushed whisper.

For a second, she considered stepping out-side. *What was he doing out there? Didn't he have a plane to catch? Or was he waiting for Mallory? Or was he watching her?* Kim focused her eyes, trying to see through the night. The figure was merely a silhouette inside the car. It may not even have been human. Possibly a coat or the head rest. Or maybe it wasn't even Addison's car at all.

She could still hear him breathing into the phone.

"Hello?" When she tried to speak, her voice wavered. "Addison?"

The line clicked and a dial tone blared.

Startled, Kim pulled the blinds shut. As the dial tone shrieked from the receiver in her hand, she returned it to the base on the end table.

She caught herself glancing uneasily over her shoulder.

I'm just spooking myself, she thought and

laughed at her uneasy nature. When she opened the blinds again, the car was gone. A moment later, a silver Porsche pulled up and parked. Mallory stepped out with Gunz Gonzales. Taking hold of his hand, she led him inside her townhome.

She'd better be more careful, Kim thought. She wondered if Addison was trying to catch her in the act.

Curling up in her old recliner, Kim sat with every light on in the townhome. She heard every creak as the old building settled and jumped each time the wind rapped on the windows. She saw faces from the corners of her eyes, but when she turned her head, there was no one there. *Ghosts*, she thought.

When the sun finally rose the next morning, Kim had been awake for hours waiting. It didn't matter. Later today, she would be reunited with Ross.

He was waiting for her.

* * * * * * *

Deep in the wooded areas and cow pastures behind the Flying J Truck Stop, police found the blue Camero and towed it away. Afterwards, four patrol men combed the lake.

The blood trail was the first indication that foul play had occurred. And searching the dark waters and swampy marshlands, two officers found the body lying face down in the brush. When they turned it over, they found Ross McGuire's corpse, stiff with rigor mortis and writhing with insects.

From his right eye socket protruded a wooden awl handle.

JC Gatlin

12
Dark Places

Friday, January 14, 2000
6:30 PM

"Oh, Ross..."

Kim sat in her bedroom and stared critically at the image reflected in the vanity mirror, wondering if she could ever look like Julia Roberts in *The Runaway Bride*. Or even *Pretty Woman*. She styled her hair for an hour before deciding to wear it down. Five minutes later, she debated whether to pin it back up again.

As her mind raced with everything she wanted to say when she saw him, her hands, hidden from sight, twisted nervously in her lap. *Where have you been? Why have you been so elusive? Will things be different now?* Then Mallory's voice echoed somewhere deep inside, saying, *"Are you sure it's*

Ross who set this up?"

Shaking her head, she abolished all the dread from her thoughts. She focused on Ross.

Zeus lay at her feet and watched her intently. She glanced down at him, then gave him a quick pat between the ears.

Moving back to the other side of the loft, she flipped through the assortment of tan and navy clothes crammed into the impossibly small four-by-two closet. She literally had nothing to wear. Sighing, she wanted to cry.

Tonight was the night, she told herself. After five weeks, four days and fifteen and a half hours, she was about to see him again. She had so much to say. So many questions to ask. But beyond that, she really just wanted him to hold her again. To make love to her. To sit up into the wee hours of the night talking about all the little things that had occurred during the day and all the little things lovers tell to each other in the night.

That's when it occurred to her. The little white chiffon slip of a dress hung limp in the closet. *She couldn't wear that, could she? Could she even wear a bra in that dress?* Kim smiled, and slipped the dress off the hanger.

It was perfect. *Ross would die when he saw her walking into the dimly lit Italian restaurant wearing this dress. Fall out of his chair, hit the floor, and die.*

Zeus cocked his head, still watching her from his position on the floor next to the vanity. Kim held up the dress for him to see.

"He'll hit the floor when he sees me in this," she told him. He let out a short whimper then yawned.

Ignoring him, Kim slipped into the dress and

adjusted the sequined straps over her shoulders. She studied her reflection in the mirror, and nodded. Sexy. Daring. So unlike anything the Old Kim would wear. It was perfect.

She shook her head again, banishing all the doubt into the darkest recess of her mind. An expression of satisfaction shined in her eyes. It *was* Ross who gave her the poetry book. It *was* Ross who was calling her. And it *would be* Ross waiting for her at the restaurant. And once he saw her in this dress, he'd be waiting for her to forgive him and take him back. Waiting to rekindle their love.

Just like she had done time and again.

Kim stepped out of the bedroom loft and made her way down the spiral staircase. Zeus immediately jumped up and followed her. A knock at the door startled them both as Zeus rushed past her down the steps and headed to the door. She cautiously walked over and looked through the peep hole.

The psychiatrist was standing on the porch. He knocked again. Hesitating, Kim sighed, glanced at Zeus then opened the door.

Dr. Whitman grinned.

"Sorry to disturb you," he said. He was now wearing khakis and a navy sports jacket. His gray hair looked natural and complimented him better than the odd colored dye. "I felt like we got off to an awkward start at the ball park."

"You don't need to apologize." She hesitated at the door. "You look better. Normal."

Dr. Whitman chuckled and ran a hand through his gray hair. He then held it up to her, revealing his palm. "No more Indian Summer," he said.

Kim smiled at him and opened the door further.

"I would offer you something to drink, but I'm actually on my way out."

"I come bearing a gift." He held up a wrapped package with a bow. She looked at it and then up at his persuasive grin. Hesitantly, she let him inside. Zeus growled and Kim pushed him away.

Dr. Whitman's mouth twitched with amusement as she tried to restrain the dog. With her other hand, she took the package. Looking at it while she struggled to hold Zeus, it was her turn to apologize. "My hands are kind of full."

He nodded and took the package from her, then ripped away the brightly colored paper. Inside a white box was a simple pink dress with hand-stitched golden glass beads. "It's for standing you up on New Year's Eve. Mallory told me that you ruined a dress that night."

"Actually the garbage disposal did." She took the dress and examined it. "But thank you. You don't know how much I appreciate that."

"Well, it's not as nice as the one you've got on." He laughed a little, then shot her a fleeting look. "You look simply stunning"

Zeus growled, threatening him.

"I have a date," she said and glanced at her watch.

"I guess you gotta be fashionable for war."

Kim glared at him. "Excuse me?"

"That was just a thinly veiled reference to our upcoming date," he said, holding up his free hand. "I'm just looking forward to our weekend warrior trip."

Zeus barked and lunged; Kim held him back.

"That does it!" She took the Doberman by the collar and dragged him across the living room floor.

Pulling him up the spiral staircase by his collar, he huffed and fought her all the way upstairs. Finally, she shoved him into the bathroom and shut the door. Zeus was howling as she turned around.

Dr. Whitman stood directly behind her.

Kim jumped, bumping into him.

"What are you..." she stuttered. "This is my bedroom."

He stepped toward her, crowding her personal space. She could hear Zeus barking and growling in the bathroom.

"It's alright," he said to her, his breath hot on her face. "Animals never seem to like me."

She gently pushed him back, away from her. He took a step backwards, giving her some space.

"I'm sorry." His voice lowered. "Am I making you uncomfortable?" He handed her the box with the dress in it. She gripped the soft fabric of the dress, letting the box fall to the floor between them. She held the pink dress to her chest, almost as if it was a shield. She suddenly felt very exposed in the thin chiffon.

"You're in my bedroom," she said again.

"Kimberly, I just want to be straight with you." He spoke in an odd, yet gentle tone. "You're a very attractive woman."

Kim didn't want to hear this. She threw the dress down. It landed softly at her feet. Moving past him, she made her way out the loft and down the spiral steps. He came down after her. At the base in the living room, he started to reach for her, then shrank back.

"I don't mean to make you feel uncomfortable," he said. "I've just been terribly alone lately. And

Addison said that you too were recently… lonely."

"I'm not lonely," she answered in a rush of words. "I'm meeting my boyfriend tonight. He's waiting for me."

"I apologize." The doctor shook his head. Now he too looked down at his feet and mumbled, "I misunderstood when Addison said….well, it doesn't really matter."

Flashing a quick smile, he made his way toward the door. "I'll just let myself out. I certainly never meant any…"

"Wait." Kim interrupted him. She suddenly realized something. Something she missed earlier. Something that superseded the awkward moment. "When did you last speak to Addison Gaynor?"

"I don't know." He hesitated at the door, as if thinking about the question. "Before the baseball game, I think. We found his wallet."

"Is he really out of town?"

"Mr. Gaynor?" he asked. "I don't know. I suppose. Do you need him? Is something wrong?"

"No." Kim wasn't sure what to say. "He said he was going out of town, but I'm not sure if he really left."

"That's odd. Why would he lie about that?"

"To keep tabs on Mallory," she said bluntly. "To spy on her."

"Is he harassing her? Or you?"

"I wouldn't take it that far."

"Think about it Kimberly," he said. "This could be serious. Has he ever mentioned having a family out of town?"

"No, not to me at least. Why?"

"He had some problems with a girlfriend, maybe

she was his fiancée by that time, I don't know."

"What do you mean?"

"I mean a few years ago he got in trouble with her when she apparently broke off the relationship. She moved out and got her own place, but Addison wouldn't leave her alone. He continuously called her and spied on her and genuinely made her life a living hell."

"Does Mallory know about this?"

"I don't know."

"We need to tell her..." Kim glanced at her watch again. "Tomorrow. Like I said, I don't want to be late."

She grabbed her coat and slipped her arms into it as she led the doctor out of her townhome. After locking the door, she faced him once again. He uncomfortably cleared his throat, as if stalling for time.

"I'm looking forward to this weekend," he said quietly. "Mallory has told me a lot about you."

"Look, I'm involved with someone." Her coolness was evidence that she was done with this conversation and he winced at her words.

"I guess that would be Ross?" he asked.

"Mallory didn't mean to lead you on. Ross and I went through a rough patch, but we're reconciling. I'm meeting him tonight."

"I didn't know."

She let out a low sigh. "I think it'd be best if you left and didn't call me again. I don't mean to be rude. Just honest."

With that, Kim turned and took a step off the porch. Dr. Whitman reached out and grasped her arm.

"Wait, Kim," he said. She hesitated and turned to him. He took a breath. "Addison has keys to Mallory's home next door."

Kim bit her lower lip, waiting. "Yes?"

"Does he have keys to your home too?"

"No," she said defensively. "Of course not."

He held her arm, just below the elbow. His grip tightened. She looked down at this hand, then back up to meet his gaze.

"Of course he doesn't," she said again.

He released his grip and Kim backed away. Turning again, she was in the parking lot headed toward the black iron security gates.

She didn't look back, though she knew the shrink was watching her. She walked faster, rushing.

Tonight, she would take the short, direct route to downtown. She wouldn't walk along Morris Munger Road or take the time to pause at the bend, to sift through the weeds and discarded trash for the lost engagement ring. Tonight there wasn't time.

Ross McGuire was waiting.

13
Guess Who's Coming To Dinner

Kim arrived at Greico's Italian restaurant promptly at eight, looking hot in chiffon and high heels. Pausing at the hostess station, she was surprised when the maitre d' exclaimed, "We've been expecting you!"

Taking her coat, he lead Kim to a table for two.

"Your party will be joining you shortly," he said, watching her. Kim stared at the table; a look of disappointment marred her face. *Where was Ross?* She turned her head, searching the restaurant. The maitre d' leaned toward her. "Is something wrong, ma'am?"

"No," she said, smiling graciously at him and sitting in the seat pushed out for her. A hundred memories flashed through her head as she remembered the night she and Ross had first sat at this exact table. It was eerie. "You said my party will be joining me shortly."

"Yes, ma'am. He asked that you forgive his lateness and said that he was unavoidably detained."

"He did?" Kim thought about that for a moment. *Unavoidably detained*, she thought then asked, "Who made the reservations? Was his name Ross McGuire?"

The waiter looked baffled. "I would have to check, ma'am. If you could be so good as to wait."

Kim agreed and ordered one martini and a Shock Top Belgian White on draft; she knew what Ross drank. Glancing at her watch, then at the crowded tables around her, Kim wondered when he would arrive. And when he did, would he be angry and loud or quiet and pouting? Would he be apologetic and sincere and plead with her not to shove him out of her life?

She imagined him gasping when he laid eyes upon her, falling to one knee, and taking her hand in his. Slipping his other into his dinner jacket, he would remove the lost engagement ring and show it to her. With tear stained eyes, he would place the ring on her finger before reciting another beautiful love poem.

Kim laughed at this. Ross would never wear a dinner jacket.

Flushed, her heart fluttering, she looked at the faces sitting at the bar toward the back of the restaurant. There was no sign of him there.

Or anywhere.

Now she wondered if he was even going to show. *Why was he hiding? Why was he doing this?*

Watching the people around her talk and eat and drink, Kim studied each face, determined to find him. She watched the dark corners of the restaurant, as if he would slip out from the shadows to greet her.

Her drinks arrived, and she waited.

There was a quiet music coming through the intercom system. Kim hadn't really noticed it, until she noticed the song that was playing. The waiter passed by the table again and she flagged him down.

"I was waiting for you to tell me who made these reservations."

"Why ma'am, I'm sorry." He looked embarrassed, and handed her an envelope. "He said he was your grandfather."

"My grandfather?" Kim wasn't expecting that and ripped the envelope open. It was another handwritten note. She read it and shuddered. "For my Darling Bonnie. You will always be my angel. Love, Daddy."

Kim dropped the note as her stomach turned. She looked back up at the waiter. "He said he was my grandfather? Where is he?"

"It was an older gentleman." The waiter looked across the crowded room and pointed. "Over there by the bar."

Grabbing her purse, she scanned the room. Toward the back of the restaurant, there was a young man. A college student. His face partly hidden behind a couple laughing and sipping margaritas. Their eyes locked. His black bangs fell into his face, and he raised a hand to flip a strand of hair out behind his left ear.

"Michael?" It was hard to tell. His face looked blurry in the crowded restaurant's dim light and smoky atmosphere.

"Michael!" she called out.

A waiter balancing drinks moved in front of her and a group of sorority girls chattering and squealing, insisting none of them had too much to drink, surrounded her as they tried to make their way to the door. Kim struggled to push her way through the crowd, struggling to keep her eyes on the blurry face.

Anxiously, she made it to the bar. But her classmate was gone, if he was ever actually there at all. She wasn't sure. The couple sipping margaritas looked up at her.

"Did you see the man sitting behind you?" she asked them.

Their heads turned and they glanced at the empty bar stool. Apologetically, they frowned at her.

Frantically searching the crowded restaurant, then sighing, Kim stepped away from the table and made her way toward the entrance. She walked through the dimly lit parking lot, glancing behind her.

There was no one there.

* * * * * * *

Kim came home that night feeling dejected. Again, she read the handwritten note from the restaurant. It definitely was not from her Grampa. Something was terribly, terribly wrong.

Was it Michael all along who was calling her, reading the Pablo Neruda poetry? Did he give her the book? She had seen him that afternoon she needed Mallory to pick-up Zeus at the campus. He was sitting on the bench next to her books, where she left them for a few minutes to meet Mallory at her car. He could have slipped the poetry book among her text books at that time. But why?

Alone, she looked at her dark living room. The shrink had been standing there a few hours ago.

Stepping upstairs to the bedroom loft, she let Zeus out of the bathroom. He greeted her as she moved to the bed and turned down the sheets. She slipped out of the chiffon dress. It dropped to the floor in a heap of fabric around her feet. Kim stepped out of it and left it there on the floor.

Ignoring Zeus, she found the poetry book lying on the night stand. She picked it up and read the inscription. *"For my Darling Bonnie. You will always be my angel. Love, Daddy."* Staring at the cursive handwriting, something else caught her eye. She turned her head.

On the night stand, sitting where the book had lain just a moment ago, where Dr. Alec Whitman had been intrusively standing just a few hours ago, was something shiny.

Very small. Very bright.

Kim leaned closer, peering at it. She blinked, not believing what she saw.

The Solitaire diamond ring with the two-tone band lay on top the nightstand. The little diamond actually sparkled, reflecting moonlight shining down from the overhead skylight.

Startled, she stepped back. She didn't breath. She couldn't take her eyes off it. *Was she really seeing what she thought she was seeing? Was her engagement ring really sitting there?* She had to be dreaming.

The phone rang downstairs, bringing her out of the trance.

It rang again.

She bolted down the spiral steps. Zeus followed. Looking behind her toward the recliner and the end table it rested on, she watched the ringing phone, wondering if she really wanted to answer it.

She started to reach for it, then drew back.

It rang again.

She picked up the receiver and slowly brought it to her ear. "Hello…"

Static crackled on the other end, then a man whispered her name. Kim sat up, almost dropping the phone.

Clearly, it wasn't Ross' voice. *Why had she thought it was all this time?* Perhaps she had simply chosen to ignore her better judgment, to fool herself into believing Ross was reaching out to her, like he had done time and time again in the past. But this voice sounded nothing like Ross' voice.

The caller continued, quietly reading 'If You Forget Me.' When he finished, Kim's eyes dropped to the floor.

"Who is this?" Her voice trembled. He remained on the line, static filling their momentary silence. "Who are you?" she asked again.

There was no answer.

"Did you have my engagement ring?"

Silence.

"How did you get in my house?"

There was a breath of reply, but no words. Static crackled in her ear again, then the voice was an articulate vigor.

"*If you forget me*
       There is something I want you to know."

The line clicked. The caller was gone. Kim hung

up the phone, questioning it all. Questioning herself.

Fear and anger knotted inside her as she picked the phone back up. She wanted to call Mallory, but remembered that she was still out with the baseball player.

Her hands trembling, she dialed 911.

It took 20 minutes for the police officer to knock on her door. Holding Zeus back, she told him what happened.

"So no one broke in," he confirmed. His voice was deep and comforting, but he made it clear that he was irritated to have to fill out another report.

"No," Kim replied. "It wasn't a break in."

"So nothing was stolen? You checked."

"Well, no. Nothing is out of place but the engagement ring, you see..."

He cut her off before she could finish. "So you found an engagement ring you lost five weeks ago?"

Frustrated, Kim asked him to listen. She told him about Ross' disappearance and the mysterious notes, about the phone calls and the dinner engagement at Greico's Italian Restaurant. And the odd boy with wavy black hair from her literature class who was watching her there and often stared at her in class. Then she told him about Addison spying on her neighbor and possibly having a key to her home, and the shrink with a bad dye job and cases of unstable patients who repeatedly caused him to stand her up over the last couple of weeks.

If the officer wrote any of this down, Kim couldn't tell. His pen didn't move across his notepad as much as she would've liked. Still he offered to check the windows, peek into the small bedroom closet and look under the bed. Zeus followed him around the townhouse with his ears perked up, checking each nook and cranny immediately after the officer.

When he finished, the officer sighed and hesitated at the front door.

"So you found an engagement ring you lost five weeks ago." His voice was courteous but patronizing. "You should keep your doors locked."

14
Death Comes Calling

Saturday, January 15, 2000
8:12 AM

"Missy, I wanted you to change the locks the minute Ross ran out of here," the landlord said later that morning, trying to be heard over Zeus' incessant barking. Kim grabbed him by the collar and held him back.

"I'm serious about that no pets clause," he said, his face partially hidden beneath his weathered straw hat. He was wearing the same old overalls he always wore, day in and day out. Zeus snapped at him and Kim apologized, gripping her dog.

"Let me just get him out of here," she said. "I'll take him over to Mallory's."

Moving past him and out the door, she pulled Zeus onto the front porch and toward the sidewalk.

He barked and howled, struggling against his leash to turn and look at the landlord kneeling at the front door behind them. Kim wondered what the neighbors must think.

She headed over to Mallory's next door, when she noticed the BMW parked near the garbage bin. It was running, facing their building. There was some one inside, watching.

"Addison," she said. Her eyes focused on the man behind the steering wheel. Dragging Zeus by his leash, she stepped off the sidewalk toward the BMW.

It rolled forward, then moved through the parking lot. Kim screamed and ran after it. Startled by the sudden yank, Zeus turned and ran with her.

"Addison," she yelled. "Addison, stop."

The freshly-waxed car with tinted windows inched forward. Its engine revved then it rolled to the security gates. When they opened, it raced out and down the street. Kim ran to the gates as they closed and watched the car disappear.

Pausing, she was certain it was Addison's BMW. He had been watching them, again. Then she turned and dragged Zeus back to the curb. A moment later, she was pounding on Mallory's door.

Her front door opened and Mallory poked her head outside. Her hair was a tangle of red, and a blue blanket wrapped loosely around her bare shoulders.

"What is it?" she asked.

"We need to talk." Kim pushed the door open and entered the living room. Clothes were strewn across the floor, and she noticed a black and white striped baseball jersey draped across the couch. A pair of cleats lay at the bottom of the spiral staircase.

She looked at Mallory.

Mallory pushed Kim back toward the doorway. "Do you ever stop to think about what's happening to others before you come barging in?"

"Mal, listen to me…" Kim pushed back against her friend. Mallory struggled to hold up the blanket as she leaned into Kim, forcing her to take another step back. Kim held up her arms, blocking her. "Would you listen to me? Just listen."

Mallory shook her head and grabbed Kim's arm. "Now isn't a good time for your drama. I have company."

"Mal, listen. Does Addison have a key to your townhome?"

"Of course not. Why?"

Kim leaned forward. "Do you have my spare key?"

"What?"

"Where's my spare key?" She raised her hand, pointed a finger. "You have a key. Where is it?"

Mallory gestured toward the door, then paused. The key hook was empty. "They're... It's gone."

"What?"

"My spare key ring. It's gone."

"So Addison has it."

"I don't know. Why would he…"

Kim interrupted her. "If Addison has a key to your house, then he has a key to my house."

"What are you getting at?"

Kim paused, collecting her thoughts, then continued. "Addison is watching you." she said, breaking free of Mallory's vice grip on her arm. "Addison is watching us."

"What?" Mallory sounded curt, evidence that

she was not amused. "He's out of town."

"No, he's not." Kim glanced at the jersey again. "I just saw him outside sitting in his BMW."

"You're being paranoid." Mallory turned her back, dismissing her. Kim started to protest but Mallory seemed bent on changing the subject.

"Besides, I've got something to show you." Gushing, Mallory ran over to the couch. She picked up a baseball bat and held it up to show Kim. He had autographed it in black marker. "Look what Gunz gave me!"

"Mal, you're not listening to me."

"It's the bat from his home run the other day," Mallory continued. "And let me tell you, Kim. This bat here, isn't the biggest bat he's got."

Kim grabbed the bat from her hands and threw it on the floor. "You're not listening to me, Mal. Addison was just here, and I think he may have been at Greico's when I was waiting for Ross. The waiter said my grandfather was there."

"What exactly are you trying to say?" Mallory crossed her arms as the corner of her mouth twisted with exasperation. "And say it quietly so that you don't wake-up the Gunz. We had a late night last night."

"What I'm saying, *exactly*, is that Addison is spying on us. Something is wrong, really wrong and I called the police..."

"You called the police?" Mallory shot a throaty laugh, clearly to cover her annoyance. "Would you listen to yourself? What I hear you saying is that Addison cares about me."

"Then why is he spying on me? Why was he at the restaurant last night and why did he tell the waiter that he was my grandfather?"

"You're getting all melodramatic again."

Mallory's chiding tone angered her, and Kim cut her off. "The shrink, er, the doctor, Alec Whitman, he said that Addison has a past of stalking some ex-girlfriend. He genuinely made her life a living hell."

"What's your point?"

"My point is that everything that's going on, everything that I thought was Ross, I think Addison is involved," Kim insisted, moving her hands to further illustrate the point. "If he was at the restaurant like the waiter..."

"I can't believe we're having this conversation again." The expression on Mallory's face bordered on mockery. "Strange phone calls. Strange notes. Exploding garbage disposals. It doesn't end with you, and now you're trying to draw my Pudd'n Toes into the middle of it."

"He found my engagement ring." Kim removed the diamond ring from her pocket. She held it up.

"What?" Mallory's eyes widened and she reached for it. Kim drew back.

"He set it on the nightstand next to my bed," Kim said, "like a display or something."

"Your ring?" Mallory couldn't take her eyes off it. "But why?"

"Because he's lying to us." Kim closed her fist, hiding the ring. She returned it to her pocket. "He's not stable. You need to cut him out of your life. Out of our lives."

"You can't tell me who to see and not to see." Mallory stepped closer to Kim, her whole demeanor was growing in severity. "Especially after I tried for years to get you to cut Ross out of your life."

"But you're dating a man that is affecting us both. A true friend would not put her best friend in jeopardy over a man."

"Don't tell me how to be friend." Sudden anger lit her eyes. "I've been a friend through this whole circus you call a life. I'm the only friend you've got."

"You are not the only friend I've got, Mallory Astin. In fact, I've lost a lot of people lately, and you're making it very easy right now to cut one more person out of my life."

"Oh that does it!" Her temper flared and Mallory leaned in toward's Kim's face. She spat out the words contemptuously. "Get out of my house!"

Mallory pushed Kim backwards toward the door. Kim resisted as Zeus barked and snapped at her.

Struggling to keep the blanket wrapped around her midsection, Mallory screamed at the dog, igniting him into a spasm of barks. Kim gripped his collar and held him back as she stepped backwards out onto the porch.

"Fine." Kim shot her a hostile glare.

Mallory slammed the door shut.

She stared at it a moment, then looked down at Zeus. He cocked his head, watching her. Kim looked back at the door as her gray eyes darkened like angry thunderclouds. Curses fell from her mouth. Tugging on his leash, she marched Zeus back to the sidewalk and around to her home next door.

The landlord was still installing the locks and he looked puzzled when Kim and Zeus raged inside. She grabbed the edge of the front door, knocking his tools out the way and slammed it shut.

Zeus whimpered and then ran up the spiral staircase. She watched the dog disappear upstairs then turned to the landlord. He looked puzzled, not sure what to say. She frowned at him, leaning against the door.

"Did you and Mallory have words?" he asked, picking up a yellow and black powered drill from the floor. There were several parts and pieces of locks scattered around the threshold. Kim noticed this, ignoring his question, and instead focused on the door.

"How many locks are you installing?" she asked him. The landlord had cut five holes in the door and installed three deadbolts, with two more to go.

"You can't be too safe around here," he said to her, holding up the drill. Removing his straw hat, he wiped the sweat from his brow. He then replaced the hat and smiled at her. "Mallory's a hot head. I'm sure you'll make up."

Kim shook her head.

"Not this time." She folded her arms across her chest and turned away. "Mallory thinks of no one but herself. She is the most selfish, self-indulgent, egotistical…"

A knock at the door interrupted her. Startled, Kim jumped. Zeus barked and scrambled out the bedroom loft and down the spiral staircase. Kim saw him and grabbed him by the collar as he rushed past.

"If that's Mallory, I don't want to talk to her," she said, holding back her dog. She glared at the landlord beside the door. "You tell her I'm not accepting her apology so she can just turn herself right back around."

As if getting a chuckle out of her theatrics, and

like any true southern gentleman would, he approached the front door and opened it. Surprised, he stepped back and opened the door wider.

Kim was about to tell Mallory a few choice words but hesitated when she saw who was at the door. Staring at two uniformed police officers standing on her front porch, Kim took a couple hesitant steps forward. Zeus barked at them.

"Excuse, Miss Bradford?" the taller one said.

Kim froze. Her heart pounded in her chest. "Yes?"

"Are you Kimberly Bradford?" the taller officer asked. Kim glanced at the landlord.

"Yes. What can we do for you, officer?" she asked, stepping forward. She held her dog back.

"Miss Bradford," he said, looking directly at Kim. "I'm afraid we have some bad news."

"What is it?"

"It's Ross McGuire. A patrol car found his body."

Kim was speechless. "What?"

"Ross McGuire is dead," the officer clarified. "And we're going to need you to identify the body."

"Ross?" The word stuck in her throat. Her heart stopped. She wasn't sure if she was hearing them correctly.

"Five weeks, five days and five hours." Her voice caught in her throat. Her head spun round. She thought she was going to be sick. She looked back at the police officer. "Five weeks, five days and five hours."

"Miss Bradford," the officer said again. "We need you to come with us."

15

The One You Love

Kim sat impatiently in interrogation room two and stared at the wall. She had been sitting in the small confines of the room since early that morning. It was late afternoon before the Detective finally told her she was free to leave.

Kim stood and slowly stepped to the door, opened it and slipped into the busy hallway of the police station.

Mallory was waiting for her, and rushed to her as Kim came through the locked doors and into the lobby.

"Oh, Kim," Mallory said, wrapping her arms around her. "I heard everything. I'm so sorry."

Kim embraced her tightly, saying nothing.

Outside the police station, Michael was waiting for them and approached the girls as they made their way down the stone steps at the front entrance.

"What happened to Ross?" There was a possessive desperation in his voice. "Tell me what's going on!"

Mallory pushed him away. "Not now..."

"Something's happened." His voice rose an octave as they brushed past him. Mallory's white Miata was at the curb in front of a parking meter. Bolting down the steps, he followed them. "I want to know what's going on."

"Leave us alone." Mallory opened the car door for Kim and placed a hand on her arm for added assistance. She did her best to shield Kim from the distraught young man.

Michael was crying now, blocking her at the car door. "Please," he sputtered. "Please..."

Kim hesitated, raising her head to meet his gaze. She wanted to say more, but her voice broke slightly. She managed a slurred rush of syllables that formed some foreign-sounding phrase. "He's dead."

It didn't even sound like her own voice. And the words were hollow, had no meaning. Kim felt like she was having an out-of-body experience, watching her mouth say those two simple words. She wasn't even certain for a fact that she had spoken them.

But Michael heard.

He stumbled backwards, speechless, tears running freely down his cheek. Standing at the curb, he watched Kim climb into the passenger seat and pull the door closed.

"He's dead..." His voice was barely a whisper.

He shook his head and wiped his eyes with his shirt sleeve as the girls sped away.

Mallory drove Kim home in silence. She wanted to talk about their fight. But it was pointless. She really didn't know what to say about it anyway.

Kim seemed so distant, lost in her thoughts, and stared out the passenger side window. Had Mallory said anything, Kim probably wouldn't have wanted to hear it anyway.

So she turned on the radio and cranked up the volume.

When they returned to the townhome complex, Kim knocked on the landlord's door. He asked about Zeus and gave her a new set of five brass keys dangling from a ring. He had installed five deadbolts into her door, for protection.

"Five deadbolts? Really?" Kim held up the key ring. "Really?" she asked again. When she got to her front door, she inserted each key into each lock and slowly unlocked her door. Zeus greeted her, jumping up and placing his paws on her shoulders.

"Do you need me to stay with you?" Mallory asked her.

Kim shrugged and shook her head. Shoving Zeus away, she stepped into her dark home.

Mallory reached for her. "Wait, Kim…"

Kim hesitated. She didn't look up at Mallory or really even acknowledge her. She just simply paused in the doorway, staring down at her tennis shoes.

"Kim, I'm just really, really sorry," Mallory's voice caught in her throat. She waited for a response, but Kim didn't give one. Finally, she continued. "Not just about Ross, but about our fight and, well, you know, about everything."

"Don't mention it." Her voice had drifted away as she shut the door on her friend. With Zeus behind her, she locked it, slowly turning each deadbolt. It took all the energy she had left and she leaned against the heavy wood casing. Her eyes tearing, she slid down to the floor and sobbed.

Zeus approached her, sniffing her cheek then licked her ear.

* * * * * * *

It was the middle of the night when Kim rose from her bed. She couldn't sleep. Zeus watched her as she dressed, grabbed her coat, and made her way downstairs. He followed. Coming to the door, she turned and told him to stay. A moment later, she was outside locking the five deadbolts.

The moon high above her, Kim walked across the shadowy parking lot and slipped through the security gates. She walked the streets, passing in and out of the glow of lamp posts, and made her way downtown. Her mind raced with memories of Ross. And, she fought back tears as she walked the empty sidewalks. The night wind screamed around her, and she buttoned her coat tighter, scrunching it around her neck.

She didn't want to go home. Walking for another forty-five minutes, Kim found herself at the old folk's home. She entered the building, the dry, hot air turned-up an extra notch on this cold January night. Stepping through the hallway, she found the night shift workers on the floor. Nurse Carla was nowhere in sight.

Kim came to her grandfather's room and creaked open the door. She peered inside. Grampa was asleep in bed. Quietly, she slipped in and shut the door behind her. Coming to his bed, she watched him a moment. He was lightly snoring. She leaned over the bed and hugged him, then kissed his fore-head.

Maneuvering through the dark room, she sat in the recliner by the window. Sitting deep in the chair, she brought her knees up to her chest and wrapped her arms around them. The window was drafty and cold, but the room was blistering hot. She could hear her grandfather a few feet away in bed, quietly wheezing as he breathed. Finally shutting her eyes, Kim fell asleep in his old recliner and dreamed about Ross.

When morning came, she opened her eyes and found her grandfather standing over her.

"Hey Princess," he said. "What are you doing here?"

She looked up at him. "Grampa?"

"Kimberly?" He knelt beside her. "Are you okay?"

"No," Kim said. She felt the tears welling in her eyes and her face flushed. "It's Ross. He's dead."

"Oh, Princess." He took her hands in his and caressed them. "Tell me what happened."

Kim felt his thin arms wrap protectively around her, and she rested her face on his shoulder. She felt thankful for his embrace and brief lucidity, just when she needed it the most.

* * * * * * *

Morning sunlight spilled into the small living room of the rental home just two blocks from the University. A faded couch with springs breaking through the fabric faced an old television set in the corner and a scratched coffee table littered with text books, notebooks, empty pizza boxes and old beer bottles.

Michael sat on the hardwood floor in front of a dying fire. He ripped another page from a spiral note book and tossed it into the glowing blaze.

A shirtless teenage boy stumbled into the living room, stretched and let out a loud sigh. He then flipped through the empty pizza box looking for left overs.

"Morning, Roomie," he muttered with half a yawn. "You been up all night?"

Silently, Michael ripped another page from his notebook. He tossed it into the fire, where the page lit up in a burst of blue-orange and disintegrated.

"What are you doing?" the boy asked him, and moved beside him by the fire.

Michael ignored him, ripping out another page. The boy grabbed it before he could throw it into the fire.

"What is this?" he asked, staring at the paper. It looked like some kind of poem in handwritten cursive letters. "Did you write this?"

Michael shot him a fleeting glare and ripped the notebook paper from his hands. He gave it a quick glance, reading a couple of lines he had written.

"For every tear that you have shed
My own heart has wept and bled."
This had been one of his very favorite poems. It was poetic. Beautiful. Sad. Lonely. And it was about Ross.

"He's dead..." Michael spat under his breath, then tossed that page into the flame. It lit up before gradually disintegrating into a wad of black ash.

JC Gatlin

16

A Grave Denied

Friday, January 21, 2000
11:38 AM

Rain made the already miserable conditions of Ross McGuire's funeral that much more unbearable. But the attendance was fairly admirable at the First Baptist Church of Stillwater. Ross came from a large family, and it appeared every relative was there. His drinking buddies and several brothers were pall bearers. Many of his coworkers left the garage early to pay their last respects. His mother sat in the front row, sobbing uncontrollably.

The service was understandably closed casket. Kim and Mallory sat with the family. She looked around at the teary-eyed faces in the little church. She was surprised to see Alec Whitman there. And, appreciated the landlord and Mrs. Roundtree showing their support. She brought little Rosie with her, and held the dog in her arms. Most surprising was her Professor, with his hands cupped in front of him, some three aisles behind her. Several of her classmates sat in the row alongside him.

Michael was among them. Quiet as ever. But his eyes weren't focused on the shiny casket, or the grieving families, or the eggshell memorandum detailing Ross McGuire's short life. He was watching Kimberly. Staring at her. Glaring at her again. Their eyes met.

Kim looked away and over at Mallory. She was searching the crowd as well, and Kim wondered if she was looking for Addison. And, she wondered, if he was here, somewhere, hidden among the mourners. She was positive that he had lied about going out of town.

* * * * * * *

In the back of the church, he watched Kimberly sitting in the front pew, sitting near the corpse's brothers, sitting beside his whore of a mother. Poor Kimberly. Poor, sweet little girl. He watched salty tears roll down her cheek. He wondered how long she had been crying. Poor child. She looked so frail. So gaunt. So unhealthy. As if she hadn't eaten in a week.

It made his own eyes fill with tears. His heart ached for hers.

Through blurry eyes, he watched her every

move. Her black hair fell onto her shoulders and down her back. It was so curly. So wild. So free. She should have worn it up. It would've been the proper thing to do. Still, he longed to touch her. To hold her. To comfort her. He wanted to take away this pain. This awful, ceaseless despair caused by such an undeserving boy.

He looked up at the closed casket. Its smooth oak sheen, nestled among wreathes and ribbons, couldn't hide the depravity that lay cold inside. That awful, awful corpse that touched his little girl. No, Kimberly shouldn't feel such anguish over such an undeserving boy.

* * * * * * *

Kim could feel him watching. Feel his eyes burning holes in the back of her head. Self-consciously, she looked over her shoulder. Michael was staring at her again, his eyes unblinking.

Uneasy, she reached over and took Mallory's hand in hers. Mallory squeezed it. She held Kim's trembling hand throughout the service. And she was still by her side when the procession moved to the cemetery, and Kim was standing over the gravesite.

The graveside services were short, as the rain kept most of the mourners away. But Michael was still there. She watched him button his black coat to keep out the rain.

When the casket was lowered and the mourners parted, a sea of black umbrellas returning to their cars, Kim let go of Mallory's hand and ran after Michael. Mallory tried to stop her, but Kim ignored her, calling for the thin boy with wet matted black hair to stop.

"What are you doing here?" she demanded.

He shrank back, as if he were surprised to have her attention. "Excuse me?" he said meekly.

"You've been staring at me through the whole service," Kim said, moving toward him. She was on the verge of screaming at him. "What do you want? Why are you here?"

"Ross was my friend." He kept his head lowered, his long bangs covered his eyes.

"Since when was he your friend? I don't think he even knew you."

"He knew me."

People stopped walking, watching them. Mallory approached and put a hand on Kim's shoulder. Kim swatted it away. She pointed a finger at Michael, daring him to retreat.

"Tell me," she said. "When were you friends with Ross? I want to know."

"No you don't," he said quietly and turned away from her. He started walking again. Kim ran after him, grabbing his shoulder and spun him around. He almost slipped in the wet grass among the head stones.

"I want to know what is going on here!" She shook him.

Mallory stepped forward to separate them but Dr. Whitman put an arm around her, holding her back. He leaned toward Mallory's ear. Kim ignored it, though. She was solely focused on Michael.

"What are you hiding?" Kim finally released him. Michael took a step back.

"Ross was my best friend. I loved him," he said.

Kim didn't want to hear it. "Since when?"

"Since before he met you." Michael turned around. His eyes welled with tears. "You wouldn't be together if it wasn't for me."

"What are you talking about?"

"All those love letters he wrote you, all those words that swept you off your feet," he said slowly. "I wrote them. He was reciting poems that I wrote, because he wanted to impress you."

"That's not true." She spoke in a suffocated whisper.

"Oh, love rips the heart in pieces and distance fills the empty creases." Michael's voice was barely above a whisper, as if his words were for Kimberly's ears alone. "So take what little comfort and solace to atone in knowing that you're not alone."

Kim inhaled as her mind struggled to wrap around what he was saying. She looked at Mallory. The doctor still stood beside her, his arm still draped around her shoulder, holding her back. Ross' mother was trembling. Her boys surrounded her. The Professor and several students encircled them. Kim turned back to Michael.

"No," she said. "No, I don't believe it."

"I think you knew." His voice was still quiet. Unnaturally calm. "I think you've always known."

"Why? Why would you do that?"

"I wrote them for him." A look of tired sadness passed over his features as tears flowed freely down his cheeks. "I wrote them for him" he said again, quietly looking down. "He gave them to you."

Kim didn't know what else to say. He was right. She did know. She had always known. And there was nothing left to say. Turning, she walked away.

Mallory called after Kim. Breaking free of Dr. Whitman's grip, she ran after her friend.

For the briefest second she thought she saw Addison amid the crowd of mourners. Mallory paused looking in his direction.

He wasn't there.

Of course he wasn't. Addison was out of town. Laughing at the thought, she called out to Kim and caught up to her standing next to Ross' grave. Taking her hand, she gave Kim an encouraging smile.

Still she caught herself glancing uneasily over her shoulder.

Doctor Whitman watched Mallory take Kim's hand as the two women stood above the gravesite.

He wondered what it was that grabbed Mallory's attention, and looked in the general direction she had been staring. He saw nothing unusual.

Alec considered joining the girls, then decided to give them some privacy. Turning his head against the rain and wind, he headed toward the parked cars.

When he heard his name called out, the doctor turned, complete surprise on his face. "What are you doing here?" he asked the slender man approaching him.

"I'm sorry to bother you doctor." The man

looked frazzled and was entirely underdressed for a funeral. "But I need to talk to you."

Alec forced a thin smile. He retained his affability but there was a distinct tone of annoyance in his voice.

"We've talked about boundaries before," Alec said to the man as they walked past Michael and headed for the cars. "You must call my secretary and schedule an appointment."

As the two men brushed past him. Michael didn't move from his spot while the rain fell harder. He watched everyone leave the cemetery one by one.

Kim was the last to leave. She returned to Ross' grave and lingered there for nearly ten minutes before Mallory took her by the hand and led her to a waiting limo.

He watched the headlights come on, pull from the slick pathway and roll away.

Finally alone, Michael walked over to Ross McGuire's grave. He stood where Kimberly had just stood, his feet covering the wet indentions in the grass where her high heeled shoes had been. He then knelt forward, the rain cold in his face, and read Ross' headstone.

"You had panache," he said out loud, almost yelling through his tears, never seeing the man behind him. A sudden, involuntary scream died in his throat as an arm wrapped around his neck and shoulders, pulling him back, and the instant flicker of pain penetrated his right eye socket.

Michael twisted his head, his eye popping and blood gushing down his face. He screamed and flailed his arms. His hand hit the face behind him; he punched a nose. The arm around his neck suddenly released and Michael fell forward, landing on the ground. He spun around and looked up. He could see out of only one eye. Rain fell in his face. Blood gushed down his cheek.

Above him, the angry man yelled, raging forward. He lifted his arm, his fingers wrapped tightly around the handle of a sharp awl. He thrust it forward. Michael raised a hand to protect himself. The spike punctured his hand and he screamed.

Thunder crashed and the man pulled back, whipping the awl out from Michael's hand. He thrust it again, as Michael's instincts took over and he rolled. The awl slashed through the air and planted into the wet ground.

Michael scrambled to his feet, too shocked to speak. He could barely see. The man came toward him. Moving backwards, Michael held up his bloody hand. The man raised the awl again. But Michael lunged forward, taking the offensive, and grabbed the assailant's legs, knocking him violently to the ground.

Thunder crashed again.

Michael stood and backed away from the man lying on the ground. Blood poured from his hand and he could feel it streaming from his eye socket down his face. He felt light headed, looked around and stumbled. The world around him was spinning.

Tumbling backwards, his head hit Ross McGuire's headstone. With one last thud, his body hit the ground, his face planted in the mud.

Blood poured out of the meaty eye socket into a pool of rainwater.

JC Gatlin

17
End in Tears

Mallory drove Kim home late that Friday afternoon. They rode in silence as she pulled into the complex. Kim rushed to find her keys and headed toward her front door. Mallory followed right behind her. Flustered, Kim inserted each key into each lock and slowly unlocked the five deadbolts. Mallory fumed.

"A crazy mental patient could rape and murder you before you ever got inside," she said.

Kim didn't answer as she opened the door, then rudely shut it leaving Mallory on the other side, outside.

Zeus was waiting for her, but she ignored him too. She was focused on the old recliner and walked straight over to the black scrapbook and picked it up. She flipped through the pages of photos and love letters. All the handwritten poems. Her tears splashed onto the pages now mocking her, smearing the lying words. Screaming, she threw the scrapbook at the wall. It smashed loudly taking a picture frame with it and split into several pieces on the floor.

Kim stared at it. She didn't move. She didn't cry. She didn't breath. She just stared. A cold hollow overtook her, like clammy hands wrapping around her whole body, and she walked up the black spiral stairs to her bedroom loft. Zeus followed her and she embraced him and dropped to the floor. She cradled the dog, holding his pointed head close to her own, and then broke down and cried.

She cried for a long time before finally falling into a light and exhausted sleep, right there on the floor.

* * * * * * *

At dusk, the rain finally let up and the grounds keeper strolled the cemetery in a white golf cart.

Pausing at the entrance, he shut and locked the gates. Getting back into the cart, he strolled along the path through the symmetrical rows of headstones. There, he noticed it: something above the ground that should have been buried beneath it.

Some fifteen, twenty yards away, two legs lay beside the headstone of a fresh grave. Had the deceased crawled out? The thought made his skin crawl. He laughed, squinting, trying to confirm what he saw in the fading light. Then he hopped out of the cart.

Moving toward the headstone, he stepped cautiously forward. He approached the legs, and found the rest of the body lying behind the cement block. It was bloody. Very bloody. And the caretaker leaned down and touched the boy.

Tilting the boy's head, he jumped slightly, shocked at the sight. It was a face with a missing eye. Rain and blood matted the boy's black hair. And he looked dead. Composing himself, the caretaker touched the boy's cheek.

Michael groaned.

Startled, the Caretaker stood. Stumbling backwards, he ran back toward his golf cart.

* * * * * * *

It had been the longest day of her life, and Kim didn't care if she ever woke up. But she did, early the next morning.

The skies were gray, the wind was howling. She dropped the blinds along the bay window in the living room and over the smaller windows in the kitchen and in the bedroom loft. Her townhome became a dark, cold tomb.

She moved slowly into the bathroom, and stared at her reflection in the mirror. She looked terrible. Her skin was blotchy and swollen. Her pores were large holes around her nose and below her eyes. Her black hair was a tangle of rats and frizz. She took an aspirin from the medicine cabinet and swallowed it, then took another.

She didn't know what time it was, but she picked up the phone anyway and dialed the nursing home. Nurse Carla answered cheerfully and sounded excited to hear from her.

"Why Miss Bradford, we were beginning to worry," she said. "We wondered what happened to you. Your grandaddy is missing you something powerful."

"I've got the flu," Kim said groggily, her throat hoarse and dry. "I won't be over to see my grand-father for a few days."

Carla made a long, dramatic Oooooo-ooooh. "Feel better, child," she said. "You know, my little boy had it last week. There must be something goin' round."

Kim gave a muffled but uninterested, "yeah" then hung up the phone. She went back to bed.

The next day, Mrs. Roundtree knocked on her door, waking her.

"Rosie and I were worried about you," she said through the door. "I made you a casserole." Kim told her and the little Pekingese to go away. And when Mallory called later that night, waking her again, Kim hung up without saying a word.

She only wanted to do one thing: lay in bed, in the dark, and sleep. She wanted to dream about Ross and remember everything about him. How he smelled. The roughness of his hands. His heartbeat thudding in her ear when she rested her head on his chest. Every little thing they had ever done and everything he had ever said to her. She didn't want to ever forget him. She knew she could never really get over him.

At some point – maybe it was still Saturday, maybe it was now Sunday, she didn't care – Kim was woken by Zeus' barking. He brought his food dish upstairs and laid it on the floor by the bed.

Wearily, Kim forced herself up and stumbled downstairs into the kitchen. She felt even worse than before. Her face was broken out. Her eyes were swollen and crusted with sleep. Her stomach felt queasy and empty. Her head ached.

She opened a can of dog food and poured it into the dish, then set it on the floor. Zeus wolfed it down, wagging his stubby tail.

Kim stumbled into the living room. The scrapbook still lay in pieces on the floor among the broken frame and shattered glass from the picture that once hung on the wall. For a moment, she wondered what had happened. Walking to it, she looked down on the pile of painted wood and glass.

The pile looked different, somehow. She hadn't noticed it at first. Part of the frame stuck up like some kind of twisted arm. Large shards of glass littered around the pieces of the wood. They had cut the photograph in the fall and Ross' face was slashed clean through.

Kim abruptly stood and looked away. Her heart pounded. She could almost hear it beating wildly with each shallow breath. Was she having a panic attack?

Calming herself, she inhaled deeply and walked to the large picture window. Gazing out, she noticed the street lamps glowing over the quiet parking lot. There was no movement in the dark. All her neighbors' cars stood in silent rows facing the curbs; their windows dark. Everyone was probably sleeping, tucked safe and secure in their homes.

Kim's eyes searched the quivering shadows along the parking lot and she tried to see beyond the iron entrance gates to the outer road. But it was too dark. Too early in the wee hours of the morning.

She wished that she could see a patrol car roll by. She wondered if they were watching her townhome. The thought comforted her. She felt a little safer.

A little.

Maybe...

* * * * * * *

Michael woke in the hospital and the first thing he noticed was his blurry vision. Equipment with flashing lights beeped constantly beside him. Bright colors were on his left, cards and flowers from his classmates. The right side of the room was black, until he slightly moved his head and saw more colors and a window. A blurry woman was standing in the corner.

"You're awake." It was his mother, and she stepped toward the bed. "Is there anything you need?"

A ragged grunt gurgled in his throat. Michael couldn't speak, he felt so weak. He turned his head so that he could see his mother better, and realized there was something over his right eye. He couldn't see out of it.

A nurse came into the room and approached his bed on the left side.

"You're awake," she said, adjusting the IV. She checked the monitor.

He listened to the beep, and it seemed to grow louder, pulsing to the beat of the throbbing in his head. She said something to his mother, but he couldn't understand what the nurse was saying; the beeping was too loud. It was the last thing he remembered before losing consciousness.

When he woke again, his hospital room was dark. He wasn't sure how long he had slept. Maybe it had been a few hours. Maybe it had been a few days. Regardless, he had slept. His dreams had been wicked though.

He struggled to sit up. The tubes hooked to his arms made that next to impossible. Looking around the room, he felt like his vision had cleared-up a little. The right side of his face throbbed, and despite the bandage, he could see little flashes of light that confused his left eye. It made it seem like fireworks were sparkling around him.

Before his eye could adjust, the door opened and light from the hallway flooded the room. Michael shut his eye. When he opened it again, he saw that the nurse had entered and turned on a small lamp over the sink and lavatory. She approached the bed.

"Welcome back," she said, smiling. Behind her,

the door opened again and two men entered the room. The nurse turned to them. "He just woke. Give him some time."

"We may not have time," the officer said.

"Well, make it quick," she said. She left the room and the taller officer approached the bed.

"How are you feeling Michael?"

Michael opened his mouth, struggling to speak. He wanted to say, *Not good.* It came out more as *Nuttt Uuggghhh.*

"Don't try to speak," the officer said. "I just have a few questions and I want you to nod, yes or no. Do you understand?"

Michael weakly nodded his head.

"Good," the officer said. "Do you know where you are?"

Again, Michael nodded.

"You're at Stillwater General," the Officer continued. "You were attacked. Did you see who attacked you?"

Michael shut his eye a moment, then nodded his head.

"Good. Did you know the attacker?"

Michael opened his left eye again, then shook his head. He barely even remembered what happened.

"Okay," the officer said slowly. He pulled a photograph from his trench coat and held it up. "Does this man look familiar? Is this who attacked you?"

Michael focused on the photo, staring at the bearded face looking back at him. It was the face of Addison Gaynor.

18

Impending Darkness

Tuesday, January 25, 2000
10:43 AM

Morning brought more rain and a loud pounding at the door woke Kim from her stupor. Zeus barked madly as she made her way downstairs to the living room.

"Who is it?" she asked pressing her ear to the door.

"Kimberly," came the voice from outside. "It's me, Mallory. Let me in!"

"Go away, Mal! I don't feel well."

Mallory pounded on the door, sending Zeus into another spasm of barks and yelps. "You open this door right now Kimberly Bradford! You've been locked in there for days," she yelled from outside.

"This is your last chance!"

Kim didn't answer, walking away from the door and back to the staircase.

"I'm warning you, Kim! I've got the landlord with me out here." Mallory's voice carried inside. Zeus barked and growled, leaping at the doorknob. Kim sulked back upstairs and climbed into bed. A moment later, a key clicked as it inserted into the lock and the landlord forced the door open.

Zeus barked and lunged at him as he stood in the doorway. Mallory leaned forward and wrapped her arms around the dog. He barked wildly and she held the Doberman tight. The landlord stepped back onto the porch, shutting the door, allowing Mallory to enter the townhome alone.

"Kim," she yelled, glancing up the staircase. "I know you're here!" Mallory stormed up the stairs and entered the bedroom loft. Kim lay face down on the bed, her back turned.

Mallory marched over to the bed, grabbed hold of Kim by the shoulders and swung her around.

"Listen to me, Kimberly. Enough is enough. You've got to snap out of this right now." She shook Kim and raised her up so that they were both sitting on the bed. Mallory placed a hand on the back of Kim's head and looked her eye to eye. "What do you always tell me? Life doesn't get easier…"

Kim didn't respond. Mallory tightened her grip around the back of Kim's head and repeated, "Life doesn't get easier…"

"We just get tougher," Kim said faintly, her voice hoarse. Then clarity filled her eyes and she leaned toward Mallory. She swallowed hard and bit back tears. "I can't believe he's gone. He's just gone."

Mallory wrapped her arms around her, caressing her hair. "I know," she said softly.

"I'm not strong. Not strong enough for this," Kim struggled to talk. She choked, then continued. "I just don't know how to take all of this. I feel like every thing is out of control."

"But it's not. You will get through this." Mallory took Kim's face in her hands and looked deep into her eyes. "I promise."

Kim looked away. "You don't understand." She gulped a deep breath, hot tears now slipping down her cheeks. Something flickered far back in her eyes and she found her voice again. "*He's* calling me."

"Who's calling you?" Mallory asked. "You're not making any sense."

"I don't know who he is or what he wants. At first I thought it was Ross but now I just don't know." She yielded to the compulsive sobs that shook her.

Mallory embraced her tightly, holding her. "Whoever it is, we'll make him stop," she whispered, gently rocking her. "I promise we'll make him stop."

That afternoon, Mallory got Kim out of the house. They parked downtown, had eggs and coffee at the Fork & Spoon, then went to the salon. Kim sulked while the woman cut her hair. Mallory pressed on, and they got manicures and ate lunch. By the time they pulled up to the mall, Kim was feeling human again. Though she wouldn't admit it.

Still, that nagging pulse running across her temples, behind her eyes, wouldn't go away. And Alec Whitman's words rang through her head.

"I've been thinking about Alec Whitman and the police. They all said that Addison has a history of stalking past girlfriends," Kim said as they wandered through Macy's Department Store. Kim held up a tan dress to her body and glanced at her reflection in the wall mirror. "I'm just saying, how well do you know him?"

"I have Addison Gaynor wrapped around my little finger," Mallory said, taking the tan dress from Kim's hands and placing it back on the rack. She then handed Kim a velvety plum backless number. "I can assure you, we have nothing to worry about when it comes to Pudd'n' Toes. He's madly in love with me."

"But what do you know of his past?" She held the skimpy dress at arm's length and then glanced at the price tag. She handed it back to Mallory. "He's divorced, right? What happened to his wife? Did he have kids? If so, where are they?"

Mallory paid no attention, directing the sales clerk to bring out some matching shoes. "I don't know where all this is even coming from."

"I'm just worried about what we don't know. There's a lot of crazy things going on around us right now and I think we need to ask some questions."

"Such as?" Mallory asked. A flash of annoyance crossed her face. Kim's response held a note of impatience.

"Such as, who was this girl who filed a

restraining order against your jealous, stalking boyfriend?"

"Lighten up. That was a million years ago."

Kim continued. "Why is he lying about being out of town? Why is he spying on us?"

"Because he's obsessed." Mallory flashed her a wicked grin. "Like I said, he's madly in love with me."

"The police are watching our townhomes, Mal. They're going to catch Addison lurking outside in his BMW."

"Oh, Sweetie... my Pudd'n Toes is harmless." Mallory laughed as a clerk brought out the shoes. She tried them on. Nodding her approval, she motioned for Kim to try on a pair. "And pick out a dress too. Anything you want. It's my treat."

"Why? You got The Gunz's platinum card or something?"

"Don't ever bring up that name again." Mallory stiffened as if Kim's question had just struck her. "Apparently he's dating Madonna now."

"The rock star? I thought she was seeing some British movie director."

"Either way, I can't compete." Mallory shrugged it off. "That's why we don't have anything to worry about with Addison."

"Mal, I disagree."

"There's nothing to worry about." Mallory said a little more forcefully than she probably intended. Smiling, she blatantly changed the subject. "Why don't you pick out something nice. I was the one hundred and seventh caller in KYGL 107's *Phrase That Pays* and I won one thousand seven dollars!"

Kim congratulated her then found a stunning white form-fitting dress, something that reminded her of Princess Di. She held it up, admiring the fabric. "This is beautiful. But Mal, I can't let you spend the money you won on me."

"Oh, go try it on. You'd look stunning in that. Besides, you're not wearing any of my clothes again." Mallory adjusted her blouse as if it'd been stretched out. "We're obviously not the same size."

Leaving the mall, Mallory took Kim to the nursing home to see her grandfather. He was having dinner in the cafeteria when they arrived. They sat down at his table and he looked up from his peas and carrots.

"Do you know my daughter?" he asked Kim.

"I do," Kim said, smiling patiently. "I'm your granddaughter."

He looked back down at his peas. "I'll have to introduce you sometime," he said, holding his spoon. It trembled in his unsteady hand, but he paid no attention. He seemed wholly enthralled with Kim, as if it was the first time he'd ever seen her. "She's about your age."

Kim looked at Mallory then back at her grandfather. She held out her hand and squeezed his arm. "I love you, Grampa," she said.

Late that evening, the girls returned to their townhome complex and entered Mallory's dark living room, their arms filled with packages.

"I can't wait to try these on," Mallory said,

dropping two sacks and four boxes onto the couch. She slipped off her high heels, ran her hands through her thick red hair and shook her head.

"Okay, but I've got to check on Zeus first," Kim said. She was definitely feeling better, and chuckled. "I can't believe we were gone all day. He's probably waiting for me with his legs crossed."

The street lamps over the parking lot shined into the living room, deepening the shadows around them and Kim reached for the light switch. Nothing happened.

"That's strange," Kim said, noticing the black, boxy video cassette recorder sitting on top the television. Its light was out too. "Did you pay your light bill?"

"I've got candles in my bedroom." Mallory pointed upstairs as she stood in the doorway. "You light some candles and then go walk Zeus. I'll wake up the landlord. Maybe it's just a fuse or something."

Mallory left, shutting the door behind her.

Alone, Kim fumbled through the dark to the spiral staircase and made her way upstairs to the bedroom loft. The moon shone brightly through the skylight, but she still had to maneuver carefully to allow her eyes to adjust.

Finding the night stand, her hands brushed a waxy candle stick. *Now where were the matches?* She opened the drawer, happening to glance out the window. She could see Mallory walking along the parking lot curb toward the landlord's residence.

She looked back. Flipping through the items in the drawer, Kim found a match book and held it up.

JC Gatlin

She struck a match. Shadows shrunk in the room
with the yellow flame and she lit the candle. She
shook out the match. That's when she noticed it from
the corner of her eye. Movement. Coming from the
closet.

She wasn't alone.

Kim swung around, and screamed. A man was
standing there. His eyes reflected the flickering
candle light, and he stepped forward. Moonlight hit
his face.

"Oh, my God," she cried. "Addison..."

19

By the Dim Grave Light

Moonlight lit Addison's face and his grin shined thin and psychotic. His hands gripped a wooden baseball bat. Three deep grooves had been cut out where Gunz Gonzales had autographed it. Looking down at it, then back up at Kim, he shook his head as if struggling to knock away pesky voices humming in his brain.

"Who does this belong to?" he demanded.

Kim stepped backwards, shaking. She straightened her back. Her bottom lip trembled. "Addison."

"I asked you a question." He was yelling now. He lifted up the bat, gripping it with two hands, knuckles white. "Who does this belong to?"

"I think you need to calm down." Kim held out her hand, palm up. "You're upset. You're emotional.

You need to take a breath and…"

"Tell me," he screamed at her, then lowered his arm. His voice tapered off as if he was holding back an uncontrollable rage. "Please."

Kim didn't know what to say. Stepping back away from him, she kept her arm extended, her hand up. His mood turning again, he grabbed her and threw her to the bed. Kim rolled off it and fell to the floor. The candle fell from her other hand and the lamp, jewelry and lotions on the nightstand tumbled to the floor with her.

"Where is he?" Addison screamed. He raised the bat again. "Is she with him?"

On the floor, Kim noticed the box of paint guns lying under the bed. She reached for them and dumped the fake artillery across the floor. She found the pink Tippmann X7 Phenum Electro-pneumatic. It was the paint gun Mallory had shown her earlier. She reached for it.

"I'm not a fool," he continued ranting. "You may think I don't know what's going on, but I do."

Kim stood up, clutching the pink rifle in her hands. Addison paused, staring at it.

"Seriously?" he asked.

"I think you need to leave." She steadied her arms, holding the gun. She aimed it at his head. Addison stepped back, sighed, and lowered the baseball bat.

"Kimberly, my intention is not to scare you," he said slowly, calmly. Then anger rose in his voice again. "But I get so god damned angry when YOU LITTLE SLUTS LIE TO ME!"

He swung the bat in her direction, hitting the vanity and smashing the mirror. Kim screamed and ducked as glass shattered. She ran to the opposite side of the room, near the window, and stood in the corner, her back to the wall. She raised the rifle again. Addison turned.

"I'm just trying to understand." He stepped in her direction. "I need to know…"

He took another step toward her. Kim thrust the rifle toward him.

"Addison, don't make me shoot you." Her voice trembled.

"I just need to know…" He shook his head disapprovingly. "Did Mallory ever love me?"

He took another step.

"I'm warning you," she said. Their eyes locked.

"I need to know the truth" he said. "TELL ME!"

He reached for her. She pulled the trigger. The gun popped and a torrent of red paint struck his face, throwing him back. He yelled and stumbled, flailing his arms. Kim watched him for a second, knowing she needed to move. To run.

He shook his head and wiped paint from his eyes. Splattered red branches marred his forehead and cheeks and dribbled out the corner of his mouth and down his chin. But his eyes were white angry balls of glass beneath a mask of war paint.

Kim threw down the gun and ran past him to the spiral staircase. He turned watching her and then wiped the paint from his wrinkled cheek with the back of his hand. She raced down stairs. Carrying the baseball bat, Addison followed.

"Don't run from me, Kimberly," he screamed, grabbing her arm at the front door. He swung her around. Facing her, he brought his face close to hers. "Is Mallory with him right now?"

Kim's back pressed against the door. Her left hand slipped behind her, her fingers wrapping around the door knob.

He squeezed her right arm. She struggled against him. His grip tightened.

"Let go of me." Panic rippled in her voice. His breath was hot on her cheek. She shut her eyes, scrunching her face. "You're hurting me."

* * * * * * *

Mallory knocked on the landlord's door. There was no answer. Knocking again, she felt the door give and peered inside.

"Hello?" she called out. Fishing for the tiny flashlight on her keys, she stepped into the dark townhome. She followed the narrow beam around the living room.

There was something cold about the whole place. The couch had a blanket and pillow piled together at one end. Stacks of paper were thrown on the floor in front of it. The cushions were so covered with newspaper clippings and shredded paper it was impossible to see the upholstery. At the opposite end of the room, she could see into the kitchen. The countertops looked cluttered. Dishes and food were scattered haphazardly in the sink. The refrigerator trays lay on the floor.

Mallory stepped up the spiral staircase into the bedroom loft. A single cot with just a mattress stood pressed against the far wall. The closet doors hung open, and inside Mallory saw what must have been twelve pairs of blue jeans overalls hanging neatly on a pole. Each looked as old and worn as the next, all were identical. There was a small desk with a computer. The monitor was black.

She glanced around the walls. It looked like a shrine. Sepia colored photographs, all aged and crinkled around the edges, pinned to the walls. In them, a teenager with flowing black hair and large eyes smiled at the camera. There were pictures of this girl with a high school boy. Intermixed with the photographs were handwritten poems. Mallory took a photograph from the wall and stared at it in awe.

The girl in the photo looked eerily similar to…

"Kimberly," she whispered. She read handwriting scribbled on the bottom edge of the photograph: *My darling Bonnie - 1974*

Downstairs, the front door closed. The sound echoed in the darkness. There was a click, then another click. Someone was locking the door.

Mallory held her breath. Turning around, she watched the swaying light of a lantern rise up the steps and the shadow of a man rose on the opposite wall. With slow, methodical footfalls, the landlord stepped into the bedroom loft.

"You shouldn't be in here," he said in a deep, hushed tone.

Mallory moved toward him. "Who is this girl in all these photos? Who is Bonnie?"

He shook his head mournfully, his eyes burning red just below the rim of the straw hat sitting low on his head. With a single quick motion, he ripped the photograph from her hands. Glancing at it a moment, he kissed it then carefully pinned it back in its place on the wall. Once satisfied, he shuddered with grief, but that gradually dissolved, only to be replaced with an eerie, unnatural calm – as if his soul had just been ripped from his body and carried away with his daughter's.

Mallory took a step backwards, pressing against the little computer desk. She suddenly understood.

"You shouldn't be in here..." he repeated, focused on the wall. He turned around, facing her. Shaking his head, he said it again. "You shouldn't be in here."

* * * * * * *

"I loved her." Addison screamed at Kim. "I loved her and she made a fool of me with that lumbering Neanderthal." He raised the bat again for emphasis and shook it at her. Surprisingly, he paused, as if a thought had occurred to him. Something he hadn't considered before.

"How many other men have there been?" he asked. Kim didn't answer. He let go of her arm and aimed the bat at her. "How many? Tell me, Kimberly.

How many!"

Kim pushed him away and violently swung the front door open. Racing outside, she rushed past the sidewalk to the parking lot toward Mallory's Miata. Addison was right behind her, the bat in his hands. Making it to the little sports car, she yanked open the door and scrambled into the driver's seat. She slammed the door shut and locked it. Addison reached the car, pounding on the windshield.

"How many?" he yelled, beating on the glass. "How many men have there been?"

Kim searched frantically for keys. She flipped down the visor. She opened the glove box. She lifted the center console. There were none to be found.

Addison peered into the driver's side window, his fingernails clawing the glass. Kim screamed. He slammed his fists against the car door, then took a step back. Raising the bat, he yelled as he slammed it into the window, shattering it.

Kim screamed again as shards ignited around her. He reached into the car, grabbed hold of her, pulled her arm out the window. She opened the car door, slamming it into him, pushing him away. Crawling over the gearshift, she climbed out the passenger side and ran away from the Miata.

Rushing to her front door, she fumbled for her house keys. They were in her pocket. As she fished them out, she hesitated and turned her head.

Addison lay on the ground. The baseball bat was beside his arm, rolling away. Sitting up, he shook his head, stunned, and struggled to get to his feet. From behind him, slipping out of the dark, Kim saw the familiar overalls and straw hat belonging to her landlord. He was approaching Addison.

She smiled, thanking God.

The landlord came up behind him. Grabbing his neck, he tipped Addison's head back with one hand and raised his other. His fingers gripped the awl, its metal spike glistening in the moonlight. Startled, Addison barked a partial *What the–* as the landlord jabbed it into his right eye.

It was one, swift motion.

The landlord stepped back as Addison's body twitched violently, his hands flailing toward the wood handle sticking out of his eye socket and pressing against his nose. A second later, he crumbled to the pavement. The landlord stood there and watched him die, then turned toward Kim.

Kim screamed. She struggled to unlock the door. She could hear Zeus behind it, barking. The landlord approached. Kim turned a lock, then another. She looked behind her shoulder again. He was on the sidewalk.

Kim turned the last lock, pushed open the door and rushed inside. She slammed it shut. Immediately she turned the dead bolts, all five of them. Her hands were shaking so that she could barely maneuver her fingers.

Zeus growled focused on the door.

Locked tight, Kim leaned against it. She inhaled deeply, rested her head against it and listened. *Was he on the other side?* It was quiet. She looked through the peep hole. The porch was dark, empty. He wasn't there.

Zeus growled.

Grabbing hold of her dog, she fell to the floor and hugged him, then rolled onto her back. She wanted to cry, and ran her hands through her hair, forcing herself calm again. Turning around, she lifted up on her hands and knees and crawled to the couch. She reached for the phone, grabbed the receiver. Her fingers pressed 911. Nothing. She panicked, glancing at the door then back at the phone. She pressed 911 again. No dial tone. The phone was dead. The line cut.

Screaming, she threw it on the floor.

There was a noise at the door, the rattling of the locks. A key inserted, turning. Unlocking. Zeus erupted into a barking fit. Kim watched him, then stared at the door. Another lock turned, and then another. Zeus jumped at the door and snapped at the handle.

The final lock clicked. The door opened.

JC Gatlin

20

Love, Daddy

The landlord stood in the doorway, yellow street lights from the parking lot bright behind him. Zeus lunged, leaping into the air, his jaws snapping toward the old man's throat.

In a single motion, he grasped the dog by the neck with one hand and raised his other to reveal the thin, needle sharp awl. Its pointed tip glistening red with Addison's blood and brain matter. He slashed the awl into Zeus' back, piercing him from his spine down to his stomach.

Zeus yelped and dropped to the floor. Kim screamed as Zeus whimpered in pain. Then he was silent. For a brief second, she wanted to run to her dog, but she held herself back, slowly looking up at the old man.

"Your dog doesn't seem to like me, Missy." He

shot her a penetrating look. Like a ghostly silhouette in the doorway, he watched her with red eyes barely visible below the rim of his straw hat. "I'm still considering adding a no pet clause to your lease."

"What do you want?" Icy fear twisted around her. "Why are you doing this?"

Stepping inside, he removed his hat. His bald head glistened. A shrill wind rushed in around him as he bent to pick-up the tool box lying on the threshold. Grasping it, he entered the townhome and shut the door behind him.

"I want to protect you, of course," he said quietly. He set the tool box on the floor at his feet so that he could lock the door. Deliberately, he turned each lock, then turned to her. He returned his straw hat atop his head. "You should have worn your hair up."

"What?" Kim's voice trembled. The whole thing was surreal.

"At the funeral. It would have been the proper thing to do." He walked to the wall where the framed photograph of Ross had fallen. Among the broken frame and shards of glass, the poetry book lay angled in pieces. He picked it up and thumbed through the pages.

"Pablo Neruda," he said. "This belonged to my daughter."

He opened the front flap, his eyes moving left to right as he read. He suddenly shut the book and stared directly at Kim. "If You Forget Me," he said. "Beautiful, isn't it?"

Kim's stomach clenched tight. She thought of

the inscription scribbled inside it. *For my Darling Bonnie. You will always be my angel. Love, Daddy.* She didn't want to believe it. "You're Daddy"

He stepped toward her. "I was wondering if you still had it. I slipped it into your books when I was fixing your sink."

"You're insane."

"It's such a lovely book. Did I tell you it belonged to my daughter. She loved poetry."

"But why? Did you…" She couldn't bring herself to say it. "Did you kill Ross?"

"I did what any father would do." He was emotionless, with no inner light in his eyes, no reflection of empathy.

"You killed him, didn't you? Didn't you?"

"He had your ring." He briefly looked away, toward the slashed photo among the broken frame. Then he turned back to Kim. "He had your ring. You kept searching for it, longing for it. I returned it to you."

"Why though? Why would you kill him?"

"Because I want to protect you." He knelt down, seemingly focused on his tool box. His hands gripped the wood handle of the awl, his fingers tightened around it. "Because I couldn't protect Bonnie."

"Protect her from what?"

"From losing her innocence. It's a father's job." He looked at the book in his hand. "But I failed. I couldn't save Bonnie's innocence. I tried. I told her to be good. But I failed." Dropping the book, he focused on Kim. His other hand gripped the sharp awl. "But I didn't fail you, Missy. I protected you. I did what any father would do."

"The Congressman?"

"He was touching you. He should've known better as should've that boy from your class. The one who made you cry at the funeral."

"Michael." The thought tore at her insides. A thousand horrid images raced through her mind at once, and she wanted to run. She wanted to fall to her knees and cry. But something inside her told her to stay calm. Struggling to steady her voice, she whispered, "What have you done to Mallory?"

"Why Missy, you're shivering," he said. "Are you cold?"

Her pulse beat erratically at the threatening gentleness in his words. He stepped closer.

"Are you afraid?" he asked.

Anxiety spurted through her. She could take it no more and Kim charged forward, then shuffled past him to the door. Frantically, she pulled the knob then realized the deadbolts were locked. She reached for the first bolt. Her hands were shaking. She couldn't move her fingers. She couldn't turn the locks. She grasped the door knob again, desperately trying to pull it open. She was crying now, and her fists pounded on the door. Without turning her head, her eyes moved and she could see him from her peripheral.

Like a motionless scarecrow, he watched her.

Part of her said run. Part of her said break a window. She screamed and pulled harder on the door knob. She twisted it, then beat her fists on the wood panels.

He was behind her now. She could feel his heavy presence and he softly touched her arm, his raw, cracked fingers grazing her skin. She froze, her back turned to him.

There was a long, brittle silence.

Finally he inched closer, his breath like ice on the back of her neck. He spoke in her ear. "That boy came running out of the forest with my naked daughter in his arms. They had been doing things in the lake. Things that scared fishes."

Kim stopped moving. She looked down at her feet. She felt the nauseating sinking of despair. His thin arms surrounded her.

"I came out of my farm house to find that boy had drowned my little girl," he said. "I forbid her to see him. But she snuck out of the house in the middle of the night. She snuck into the woods with that boy, shuck her clothes and Lord knows what they did before His almighty mercy ripped her soul from this earth."

Slowly, Kim turned. She lifted her chin, meeting his gaze straight on. Their eyes locked. Her heart pounded, her legs about to collapse.

"I couldn't protect her," he said again, quietly, softly touching her hair, patting her head.

She crouched back against the door. "What do you want?"

"To protect you." He enveloped her. He stood with his body against hers, his face near her face, his breath moistening the soft skin above her ear.

"You're insane." She turned her head.

He inched closer. "I'm a father."

She closed her eyes, drew a breath.

He lunged for her, grasping her by the neck with one hand and pulling her away from the door.

She struggled with him, trying to break his grip from her throat. His hands tightened. His thumb pressed her larynx. His right hand raised the awl.

"But I'm getting old and tired, my dear, sweet Missy, to truly protect you." He spat through his teeth, as if it caused him pain. "My days are growing short. And, I have to save your soul before it's too late."

"No..."

"I couldn't save Bonnie's, but I can save yours."

"Please..." She grabbed his arm with her hands, struggled to hold back the glistening spike. "I love you," she suddenly cried. "I love you, Daddy."

He moved his arm, lowering the awl.

"Daddy, I love you." She fought to control the spasmodic trembling within her, and the tension dissolved from her face. "I love you and I've missed you."

He studied her, his red eyes piercing hers.

"I know I hurt you, but you were right." She spoke slowly, her hands wrapping around the arm gripping her neck. The grip loosened. A glazed look of despair spread over his face.

"You were right," she continued. Her hand moved to grip the thin straps of his overalls, then her fingers reached down toward the clasp. "I should've never been out that night at the lake, sneaking off with that boy. You told me and I disobeyed you. I won't ever do that again."

This seemed to confuse him.

"Are you playing games with me?" He hesitated as if momentarily considering her sincerity.

"No." She forced remote firmness in her voice. "No more boys."

He let go of her neck; his eyes filled with tears. "You love me? After everything I've done."

"You were protecting me," she said. "Like a father."

He stepped closer and touched her cheek. "Then give me your hand," he said, and took her hand in his.

She looked into his wrinkled face, his tattered straw hat. His eyes were lowered, focused on her outstretched palm. He raised his hand that gripped the sharp awl. She began to shake as fearful images built in her mind.

The needle-like tip sliced into her open palm, across the deep love lines from her thumb to her pinky. Kim cried out, struggling to free her arm.

"You had to be punished" he said to her. Now instinct took over. Kim lifted her knee to his groin and pushed him away. The old man screamed in pain and flung the awl at her head. She ducked. The awl hit the wall above her and splintered the wood casing.

He lunged forward in the confusion, the straw hat flying off his head, but Kim was ready. She stumbled over him and ran. She leapt up the stairs.

Panic like she'd never known before welled in her throat as Kim rushed into the loft and headed to the window along the northern wall. Her hands hit the glass, forcing it open. She looked out, searched for an escape route. But there was no access to the roof and it was a straight drop to the ground below.

She turned away from the window toward her small closet. *There had to be something inside it to use as a weapon.* She was only halfway to it when she heard approaching footsteps. The heavy, urgent tread vibrated the wrought iron of the staircase.

Kim threw open the closet doors, shoved through the cramped clutter of jackets and blouses, pushed boots and pumps aside. *Nothing.* She didn't even have a wire hanger – they were all solid plastic.

Frustrated, she dropped to her knees.

Crouched in the corner of the small closet, she was barely hidden. But she was out of options. It was all she could do.

At the top of the staircase, the footsteps stopped.

Kim listened. Her back in the corner, she wriggled as deep as she possibly could among the assorted shoes and hanging shirts. A belt hung down over her shoulder like a slithering, black snake. She swatted it away when she noticed a shimmering sparkle on the floor a few feet away. It was her diamond engagement ring, twinkling in the light falling from the skylight above. The diamond looked like a star that had fallen to the earth and landed in her bedroom loft, where deep shadows filled the room and hid the corners in blackness.

The floor squeaked.

Kim couldn't see him, but she knew the landlord now stood just inside the threshold. He wasn't moving, evidently surveying the room. He would see an unmade bed with frilly pillows arranged against the headboard. There was a vanity cluttered with make-up and hair products. And of course the closet.

A shadowy mass moved to her left deeper into the room, and Kim's eyes widened to follow him. He stepped to the bed. Hesitated.

"Missy, I'm old. Death stalks me." His voice was almost an affront to the silence. His words piercing. "I won't be able to protect you, so you understand this is the only way…"

He walked around to the other side of the bed. From the spiked awl in his right hand, a fat red droplet fell to the carpet. *Plop.* Then another, and another. *Plop. Plop.* Blood. Her blood. She looked at the cut on her hand. She didn't have time to think about that now.

Kim turned her head, slightly straining her neck, to keep track of him.

"Don't be frightened," he said. She didn't fail to catch a note of empathy. He spoke slowly, spacing his words evenly. "Death is a natural part of life. In death, you will always be young and beautiful."

Kim tried not to listen, to keep him out of her head. She was half deaf anyway, with one ear pressed tightly to the rough sheetrock of the closet wall. Clothing weighed heavy on her back and pressed against her sides. Her chest barely had room to expand, barely accommodating her own shallow breaths. The drumming of her compressed heart against her breastbone beat so loudly in her ears, it seemed to fill the claustrophobic confines of her hiding place to the point she was certain the landlord would hear.

He turned his head toward her direction, and stepped toward the closet. Another red droplet fell in front of his boot, as he raised his arm, positioning the spiked awl. There was a mournful longing in his voice, like that of a father who must put down the beloved family dog.

"In death, you will always be innocent." His voice faded, losing its edge. "In death, you will be safe."

Kim shut her eyes, summoning her strength, trying not to think about the sharp tool from which the blood dripped. She struggled to keep her fragile control.

Taking a quick, sharp breath, she opened her eyes again.

The landlord was standing in the ray of moonlight cascading down from the skylight. He bent at the knees, studying the sparkling diamond on the floor. He picked it up.

It was the opportunity Kim was waiting for.

Leaping up from her crouched position, she spun out of the closet and slammed him in the midsection. Wrapping her arms around his waist, she threw her weight into him and they fell to the floor. He rolled on top of her, grabbing her throat. She bit into his arm. Shrieking, he let go, falling sideways.

Kim rolled on top of him and reached for the handle of the awl. He caught her wrist and bent her arm back. She screamed, punching him in the face with her other arm. Twisting, he rolled her over and straddled her, pinning her to the floor.

She could see the awl laying near her on the floor. She reached for it, stretching her arm till the tendons burned taught. Her fingers grasped the wood handle. He reached over, on top of her, and took the sharp tool from her grasp.

"I failed Bonnie." He leaned forward, speaking in her ear. "But I won't fail you."

Kim struggled but he overpowered her. He leaned forward on top of her, bringing his face closer to hers, his breath tingling her cheek.

"You understand, Missy," he said. "This is the only way I can protect your innocence."

Kim turned her head to the side, her cheek pressed to the carpet. Her face contorted as she fought against him, her eyes desperately searching for something. Anything.

"I will make it quick and painless." His weight shifted on top of her. She could hear him but his voice sounded disconnected from his body. She watched his lips move. "I want you to know this will hurt me more than it hurts you."

He shifted his weight again, restricting her breath. Gasping, she looked up at his arm. He raised it above his head. His hand gripped the awl. He pointed the silver spike downward.

A flash of motion came up beside him and the

JC Gatlin

old man's face twisted to the side, at the same time
surprised and confused. He never saw the wooden
baseball bat slam into the side of his head, smashing
his face and breaking his jawbone. His whole body
flung to the side as blood, spit and teeth exploded
from his mouth like shrapnel and embedded into the
wall. The old man slumped forward, landing on top of
her. Blood spilled out his nose and mouth.

Kim exhaled.

Standing above them, a red headed woman
firmly gripped a baseball bat.

"Yeah," Mallory said, panting. "That probably
hurt too."

Kim rolled the old man off her. His blood
splattered her shirt, arms and face. Mallory helped
her to her feet.

The room fell silent again.

Mallory stood over the body.

"The old landlord? Really?" She looked at Kim.
"We should've seen that coming a mile away."

Drawing a breath, Kim took the bloody baseball
bat from Mallory's fixed grip and set it on the bed.
Gunz Gonzales' autograph was slightly smudged with
a bloody print. It made her smile, then she looked
down at the body.

"We just get stronger." Kim clenched her jaw to
kill the sob in her throat.

There was a pool of blood at her feet, streaming
toward the engagement ring still lying a foot away.
The diamond sparkled and Mallory reached for it.

"Leave it," Kim said, taking Mallory's hand.
Together, they moved out of the loft.

Once downstairs, Kim gingerly lifted Zeus into her arms. He was bleeding. But, she could feel the faint murmur of his heart. It made her eyes tear with an equally faint glimmer of hope.

There wasn't much time.

Mallory took the hand-stitched quilt from the back of the recliner and handed it to Kim. She tightly wrapped the dog and held him close. A large brown eye flittered opened and looked up at her. Kim smiled and ran a hand over his head and massaged the skin between his ears.

Calmly, she stepped out the front door and carried him out of the townhome. Mallory followed.

They waited for the ambulance. When it arrived, its bright red-orange lights and shrill siren interrupted the night and brought the neighbors to their windows and front porches. Mrs. Roundtree was there holding her Pekingese in her arms. Kim handed Zeus to the paramedics in the back of the ambulance.

As the police arrived in a swarm of squad cars, Kim painfully climbed inside the ambulance and sat next to her dog. Mallory grabbed her hand and squeezed it. Their eyes locked, but there was nothing left to say.

After a few moments, Mallory let go of Kim's hand. The paramedics shut the doors and the ambulance moved forward through the open security gates, then disappeared down the street.

About the Author...

JC Gatlin lives in Tampa, Florida. In addition to regular fishing trips, he wrote a monthly column in New Tampa Style magazine, then began penning several mystery suspense stories. His first, 'The Designated Survivor,' was published in 2013.

He also maintains a mystery writing blog at www.jcgatlin. com

Solve the mystery

For a limited time, you can get a FREE copy of **The Designated Survivor** -- a stand alone Road Trip Mystery – direct from my website: www.jcgatlin.com.

www.JCGatlin.com

THE **DESIGNATED** SURVIVOR

A ROAD TRIP MYSTERY

JC GATLIN

YOUR FREE BOOK

★★★★★

"Fast paced action! I couldn't put this one down. Every time I thought I knew what would come next, the plot would twist and surprise me right to the end."

www.ingramcontent.com/pod-product-compliance
Lightning Source LLC
Chambersburg PA
CBHW070616130626

46556CB00001B/389